Reading
BOROUGH COUNCIL

Reading Borough Libraries

Email: info@readinglibraries.org.uk
Website: www.readinglibraries.org.uk

Reading 0118 9015950
Battle 0118 9015100
Caversham 0118 9015103
Palmer Park 0118 9015106
Southcote 0118 9015109
Tilehurst 0118 9015112
Whitley 0118 9015115

Author: PANTER-DOWNES, MOLLIE
Title: GOOD EVENING MRS CRAVEN.

Class no.

To avoid overdue charges please return this book to a
Reading library on or before the last date stamped above.
If not required by another reader ____ ___ __ _____ by
personal visit, telephone, post, en____

Published by Persephone Books Ltd 1999

Reprinted 2002 and 2005
and as a Persephone Classic 2008,
reprinted 2009

These stories originally appeared in *The New Yorker*

© 1999 The Estate of Mollie Panter-Downes

Preface and Afterword © Gregory LeStage 1999

Typeset in ITC Baskerville by Keystroke,
Tettenhall, Wolverhampton

Printed and bound in Germany by GGP Media GmbH
on Munken Premium (FSC approved)

ISBN 978 1 906462 01 7

Persephone Books Ltd
59 Lamb's Conduit Street
London WC1N 3NB
020 7242 9292

GOOD EVENING, MRS. CRAVEN: THE WARTIME STORIES OF MOLLIE PANTER-DOWNES

with a new preface by

GREGORY LESTAGE

PERSEPHONE BOOKS
LONDON

CONTENTS

⌒⟩∞∞∞⟨⌒

Preface

Letter from London 3 September 1939

Date with Romance 14 October 1939   1

Meeting at the Pringles' 6 January 1940   7

Mrs. Ramsay's War 27 January 1940   15

In Clover 13 April 1940   21

It's the Real Thing This Time 15 June 1940   29

This Flower, Safety 6 July 1940   35

As the Fruitful Vine 31 August 1940   43

Lunch with Mr. Biddle 7 December 1940   51

Battle of the Greeks 8 March 1941   59

Fin de Siècle 12 July 1941   67

Literary Scandal at the Sewing Party 6 September 1941   77

Goodbye, My Love 13 December 1941   85

War among Strangers 17 January 1942   95

Combined Operations 29 August 1942   105

Good Evening, Mrs. Craven 5 December 1942   113

The Hunger of Miss Burton 16 January 1943   123

It's the Reaction 24 July 1943   133

Cut down the Trees 4 September 1943   145

Year of Decision 29 April 1944   155

The Danger 8 July 1944   167

The Waste of it All 16 December 1944   177

Letter from London 11 June 1944

Afterword

PREFACE

⌒⟶∞∞∞⟵⌒

The publication of these short stories marks sixty years since the outbreak of the Second World War. They make a resonant duet with Mollie Panter-Downes's collection of wartime 'Letters from London', fortnightly reports that she dispatched between 1939 and 1945 as *The New Yorker's* correspondent in England.* The short stories, which have never been collected before, are arranged in chronological order as they appeared in *The New Yorker*. They are bookended by two of the Letters, one signalling the beginning of the war on 3 September 1939, the other, on 11 June 1944, heralding the beginning of its end on D-Day.

All twenty-one stories appeared in *The New Yorker* between October 1939 and December 1944; that is, approximately one every three months. Such productivity for a fiction writer is noteworthy in itself. Then consider that Mollie Panter-Downes also published 18 long articles and 153 London Letters (1,500 words per week for the latter) during the same five years. One additional biographical fact makes her accomplishments even more remarkable – and apropos to the

* See the Afterword for a further discussion of her relationship with *The New Yorker*.

modern woman. When she began to write exclusively for *The New Yorker* in the late 1930s, her life evolved into two separate and distinct strands, as a professional and very disciplined writer, and as a wife and mother, living in the country, gardening, and mixing with a wide circle of friends. She was different from two other female journalists of her time, the magisterial and intellectual Rebecca West and the dashing, worldly Janet Flanner. She was, as a long-time friend and editor portrayed her, 'a completely domesticated reporter.'[1] Her remarkable 852 contributions to *The New Yorker* – penned from a secluded writing hut in the garden of her idyllic country house – attest that she skilfully plaited the two strands of her life for fifty years.

Wartime was a period of intense and varied creativity for her. She was in her prime and bristling with the writer's powers of perception. She was looking outward when the British populace and its writers, out of necessity, were focused inward. One critic described the collective standpoint of women's wartime fiction as 'one in which no one has the emotional energy, or the time, to understand anyone else.'[2] By contrast, Mollie Panter-Downes directed her resources towards others. What she observed and felt filled her with more to say than journalism would allow. She needed other, new forms of expression.

The quotidian lives of Britons were her abiding interest, and she sought to render them faithfully in both the London Letters and her short stories. It is perhaps the one aspect of her writing on which she would choose to be judged. She said of her wartime work: 'If the pieces had value, it's because I

took note of the trivial, ordinary things that happened to ordinary people.'[3] With the quotidian as their point of departure, her journalism and short stories take two different directions. Her Letters examine daily life in its relationship to the physical and political events that hang over it in plain truth and in the abstract. Her stories, on the other hand, venture beneath the everyday to reveal the mindscapes of individuals reacting to wartime conditions.

Although Mollie Panter-Downes had published a few short stories before 1939, she seems to have come into her own with the form during the war. Her concentration on the personal and particular is well suited to the magnifying lens of the short-story form, which, by its very shortness, draws the reader's attention to detail. Being short in length and immediate in impact, it was well suited to the constraints of everyday life in wartime. H. E. Bates believed that 'if the war . . . produced nothing else in the way of literature it would certainly provide a rich crop of stories'. He predicted that the exigencies of war – dislocation, widening and deepening personal experience – would favour 'short stories rather than novels for the good reason that at such a time of crisis the physical effort of producing the shorter form must inevitably make it the more probable and acceptable medium of the two'.[4]

In her stories, Mollie Panter-Downes tends to seek Edgar Allan Poe's 'unity of impression', to wring out a certain unique or single effect. She does not seek the multiplex narrative, that which runs on a medley of modes and messages. She writes in the realist, as opposed to modernist, tradition. That

is, she favours character and 'story' over the lyrical sketch and the storyless, 'eventless becoming' pioneered by Chekhov, Katherine Mansfield, James Joyce, and Virginia Woolf – then imitated by many during the 1920s and 1930s. For her, character tends to take prominence over atmosphere and mood. Accordingly, she renders atmosphere as an externally- (versus internally-) generated state. A character's contingency to her physical locale and social milieu – rather than her situation regardless of them – is a relevant aspect of her characterisation. In most respects, Mollie Panter-Downes prefers the concrete and objective over the symbolic and subjective.

Her realistic mode, however, is more akin to journalism than to the tradition of realism in English Literature and, in order to characterise her short-story art, it is necessary to understand how it cross-pollinated with her fact-writing. She was able to strike precise, but different, balances in her fiction and non-fiction. Her humanity and neighbourliness quietly declare themselves in her reporting; her objectivity and skills of observation underpin her fiction. In the short stories, her point of view is closely related to that of the traditional journalist: maintaining a diffident presence, sensed but not declared, and pivoting on assessment and insight. She takes her position in order to observe, not to participate. Her comment on the geographical seclusion in which she wrote also applies to the position of her narrators: 'I write from a little distance'. Point of view rarely shifts or dislocates in her stories. The typical fiction-writer's self-interest is not evident. It is not an accident that there are no first-person

narratives here. Her characters get on with the hard business of physical and psychological survival during wartime. Their social and political positions are secondary. Resistance and escape come in the form of dealing directly with domestic minutiae, petty practicalities and what impedes them – not in soaring into fantasy or sinking into self and its dark abstractions.

She presents her characters without sentiment or melodrama; irony and comedy are preventive measures against them, too. For example, she inverts the notion of wartime 'emergency' in the lightly comic 'Lunch with Mr Biddle'. Mr. Biddle – social butterfly, name-dropper, and irrepressible host – is gratefully relieved of the embarrassment caused by an argument between two of his luncheon guests when he is suddenly called away to perform his duty as an air-raid warden.

The reality of wartime was so comparably unreal that realism in fiction was utterly apt. Within the context of war, the most mundane rituals expand geometrically in their significance. Witness the contents of Anne Boston's anthology of wartime short stories by women, *Wave Me Goodbye* (1989). Many of the stories by writers like Rosamond Lehmann, Barbara Pym, Jean Rhys, and Elizabeth Taylor, among twenty-eight others, border on journalism. Mollie Panter-Downes is clearly of this school. Unlike her contemporaries Elizabeth Bowen, Sylvia Townsend Warner, and Anna Kavan, she does not venture into ghost, fantasy, or the surreal.

Her best stories are less about events than they are about conditions. They do not depend on conventional

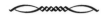

action-driven plots because their sphere is psychological, emotional and social. Neither the Blitz nor death happen in her narratives, only the anticipation or aftermath of them – unlike Rose Macaulay's fine 'Miss Anstruther's Letters', which deals directly with physical and personal destruction. For Mollie Panter-Downes, pivotal 'happenings' are internal shifts in mind, mood and heart. So, in war, waiting – for bombs, for a husband to return, for an evacuee to leave – is pure action without motion.

In these cases, one can see war as the ultimate structuring force. The stories fortify each other with their shared context. They are brief, dramatic – and comic – testimonials to the ordinary English women who did not fight in the war, but lived through it as acutely as any soldier. They are representative of the 'other' war fiction, not written by and/or about men in uniform and in action, but by women for whom war was often a completely different experience, despite the proximity of death. It is necessary to remember that more British civilians were killed than soldiers between 1939 and 1941. Therefore, one must read them as war stories, not simply as stories written during the period, 1939–1944. In this sense, they make an important claim within war literature: that wartime experience is not a male franchise. Because they are an altogether different kind of war story – a woman's – everything is changed, particularly how one should approach them sixty years later. Women writers evoke war, in the words of Elizabeth Bowen, 'more as a territory than as a page of history'. Mollie Panter-Downes evoked war in two modes. If each of her Letters from London between 1939 and

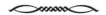

1945 is 'a page of history', then her wartime short stories are, indeed, 'a territory' – or a map of feelings, emotions, and attitudes peculiar to a British woman.[5]

Of necessity, her London Letters sprawl across a range of subjects, settings, and themes; but her stories she drew most often from her other self, the one that flourished in her sixteenth-century house near Haslemere, on the Surrey-Sussex border. There she was less the intrepid journalist than the civilian, neighbour, friend, intimate – and she wrote from these privileged viewpoints. She favours certain settings, themes, and characters. Houses are often her chosen nucleus, their significance extending concentrically into country towns and villages. The stories are peopled with housewives, widows, evacuees, billeted soldiers, and Home Front volunteers. Issuing from them are themes emanating from women's experiences in a country at war: absence, loss and loneliness, human relations under stress, social upheaval, the tragi-comedies of Englishness.

War is the primum mobile in all twenty-one stories. It is the inescapable subject. In 'Fin de Siècle', Ernestine observes that

> There was no conversation that wasn't about the war. People talked only of themselves, their jobs, their bombs, their version of [a] new 'we'. She tried to remember what they had talked about before the war. She couldn't.

Each story is a war relic: fragments of domestic life, of social detail, of feelings peculiar to, or enhanced by, war.

Collectively, the stories provide a museum piece which is evocative through its emphasis on the personal and particular, the memorabilia of gas masks, evacuees, rationed chocolate, and air-raid sirens. None of the characters is involved in active service. These are perspectives from the home front, where people suffered casualties, misery, and displacement. Here war is less about progress on battle lines than about the daily struggle to keep homes, families, and relationships alive. They offer a vivid glimpse into the special circumstances of wartime; not only physical conditions, but, above all, Bowen's 'territory' of emotions and attitudes. Because many are written in a journalistic vein, they are sufficiently extraordinary to accrue their own emblematic significance. Reading the stories, one is struck by the overwhelming immediacy of wartime living, the dislocating casualness of relationships, of people thinking about what had in their previous lives been unthinkable.

That the stories depict the misunderstood and unsung domestic side of war makes them always bittersweet, never heroic in the traditional sense. Victories come in the form of commiseration or the comfort of shared experience. Defeats are oblique; they are feelings of frustration, helplessness, and news of death that occurred weeks, sometimes months, before. Women were in the wings as understudies in the theatre of war. They were the grievers, not the grieved; the absented, not the absent. Women were charged to keep things the same, men to change things. Most of Mollie Panter-Downes's protagonists are women, but when she does feature a male main character, as in 'It's the Real Thing this

Time' and 'Year of Decision', he operates from the same position as his female counterparts: of *not* being in the war. He attempts to deal with the effects of this state on his daily life and psychological well-being.

Mollie Panter-Downes portrays a kind of heroism defined by and for upper-middle-class English women. Stoicism, kindliness, reliability, and humour prove themselves on the fields of the domestic and personal. Responding to crisis, her characters make desperate, but quiet and steady, efforts to maintain equilibrium – and to be seen to do so. There is an essential Englishness that pervades, from narrators' voices to characters' reactions. For instance, despite the conditions, her protagonists do not break down or slip into madness, like those in Jean Rhys's 'I Spy a Stranger' and Anna Kavan's 'The Face of My People'.

A comparison of Dorothy Parker's 'A Lovely Leave' and Mollie Panter-Downes's 'Goodbye, My Love' throws the latter's Englishness into relief. Two women, one American, the other English, wrote short stories for the same magazine at the same time on the same subject. From the wife's point of view, both stories address the psychological permutations that affect a marriage under the strain or prospect of separation. When her husband's twenty-hour leave is suddenly cut to one, Parker's wife explodes with the arsenal of feelings that had been smouldering for six months. Crushed with disappointment, she puts them both through a cycle of anger, frustration, bitterness, and relief. In 'Goodbye, My Love', Ruth silently struggles to prepare for her husband's departure for war; when he leaves, she anguishes in solitude.

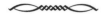

Her efforts to express herself are inadequate. When she speaks to her maddeningly reticent mother-in-law, her stiff upper lip trips a memory and an insight on British character: 'As she hung up the receiver, she suddenly remembered a French governess out of her childhood who used to rage, weeping with anger, "Oh, you British, you British!"' Just when Ruth has come to terms with the situation, her husband calls to say that his departure has been delayed and that he will be returning home for ten days. Hanging up the phone, her trusty English resolve cracks and she expresses herself for the first time – albeit in private – by bursting into tears as the story ends. In this way, Ruth 'embodies the quintessential mixture of resignation, unspoken patriotism, and quiet despair that seems to stand for British Everywoman in wartime.'[6] At century end, these characteristics, once associated with Englishness, seem long forgotten amidst post-colonial tendencies to debunk, criticise, and apologise for them as symptoms stemming from a range of cultural ills, from social repression to imperialism. Here they are lines in Mollie Panter-Downes's ode to the British woman. But this collection is not an elegy. There is social criticism, too.

Her fictions embody, give voice to, observe from, and examine the middle-class milieu at a time when serious literature and art had moved to represent and depict the poles. As a result, the predicaments and anxieties of those living in this stratum have often been dismissed as trivial compared to those of the attenuating aristocracy and the rallying and rising working classes. Mollie Panter-Downes does not apologise for her territory and the issues and

characters that occupy it. But by no means is she deferential to the middle- and upper-middle-class women who feature prominently in her stories. As they endure the discomforts of social change – a Home Front flashpoint peculiar to their class – their behaviour is as often poor as it is decent.

In attitudes and in fact, the signs and symbols of social change abound. Women's roles are reversed, standards erode, signposts are removed from country lanes, houses are dirty and in decay – for they symbolise Mollie Panter-Downes's most subtle renderings of the inevitability of social transformation and the fruitlessness of efforts to waylay or deny it. Seeking safety from the Blitz in the countryside, an old woman has left her house in Belgravia. She frets over 'the gradual disintegration of her property':

> Although the rooms had been put away carefully under dust sheets, their contents packed in newspapers or tenderly wrapped in baize, the dust had probably seeped in to lie in the dulling mahogany curlicues of the Chippendale chairs, the Georgian silver must be tarnishing slowly, the china cupids acquiring a film of grey on their dimpled pink thighs.

Perhaps Mollie Panter-Downes's finest interpretation of this theme is 'Fin de Siècle', in which she employs alternating points of view to represent a husband and wife's individual and collective pasts and attitudes becoming lost in war's wake. At the centre of the story is a derelict Art Deco house radiating with significance.

In her characters, Mollie Panter-Downes often represents two points of view – that which accepts the irreversible dissolution of certain class distinctions, and that which resists or rejects it. All classes are subject to comedy and irony, sympathy and praise. In 'This Flower Safety', the grand Miss Mildred Ewing is so rooted to her status and the accoutrements that exemplify it, that she suffers grievously when she and her maid, the resilient Sparks, move from house to house. 'Cut Down the Trees' inverts these roles. Forty Canadian soldiers are billeted at the large country house of Mrs. Walsingham. Her ageing maid, Dossie, sees these men and the war as a 'conspiracy against [her] way of life'. With her 'full and ungrudging faith in the resiliency of the British upper class', Dossie waits impatiently for the resumption of things as they were. She is annoyed by Mrs. Walsingham, who seems to embrace the shifts in their daily lives. To meet the soldiers' increasing need to store their heavy equipment, they are forced to cut down some ancient trees that once dominated the view from the house. The trees and the view are metaphors for a passing England, a change which Mrs. Walsingham accepts, even welcomes. Hers is the new attitude. Looking out of the window, she says:

> To tell you the truth, I think it's an improvement – lets in more light and air. It's altered the view from this side of the house, but what's a view? Everything else is changing so fast I suppose we shouldn't bother about trees and water staying the way they were.

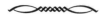

happened'. What happens when one becomes accustomed to loneliness? In 'The Waste of It All', Frances forgets what her husband looks like and grows more familiar with life without him than with him: 'Now her loneliness was something which she put on automatically when she got up and hardly noticed any more.' She became

> used to the light clip of feminine conversation, to light eating on trays. When a man came to the house, his voice seemed to roar like a giant's and the floors seemed to shudder under his unaccustomed tread.

The arc of her isolation goes so far that she constructs a husband and marriage out of memory and imagination. She takes in a village girl and her illegitimate infant, then fabricates a 'home' by buying a puppy and pretending that the baby is hers. The self-deception is fragile and everything goes wrong.

What happens to human relations when the air-raids stop? At the beginning of 'It's the Reaction', Catherine Birch is on the verge of a breakdown. Her struggle to cope with the pressures of wartime London is made worse by her inability to connect with people. Unmarried, middle-aged, and alone in her tiny flat, she pines for Blitz conditions because they brought out a 'wonderful new friendliness' and put her into intimate contact with her neighbours. Sheltering together, they were like 'one jolly family', like 'old friends', but, when the bombing stopped, they returned to their formal, private ways. She becomes painfully conscious of the double irony that a catastrophe is required to lower the most basic social barriers – and that while catastrophes are temporary, the barriers are permanent. Despite her revelation and the depths of her loneliness, she plays her part in perpetuating the condition because she, too, is incapable of reaching out. This story is perhaps Mollie Panter-Downes's most trenchant portrayal of the British character.

The effects of food rationing were ubiquitous in the 1940s, hunger most of all. In 'The Hunger of Miss Burton', Mollie Panter-Downes draws out the condition's metaphorical potential. For Miss Burton, a school teacher headed for spinsterhood, hunger takes the form of 'a wolf . . . under the neat waistband of her tweed skirt.' She simply cannot get enough to eat. She also craves love, but is forced to feed on the twenty-year-old memory of Emil, her dead German lover. Like the meagre portions of school food, this does not sustain her. When faced with the happiness of her colleague, Margaret, who is recently engaged to a soldier, her hunger distorts into austerity, envy, greed, and self-pity. Ironically, Miss Burton feels 'full' with *schadenfreude* when she suspects, at the end, that Margaret's engagement has been broken off.

The short-story genre prospers in times of social upheaval, giving voice to 'submerged populations' – those who are marginalised, alienated, or simply unseen and unheard amidst the disorder: it is in the modern short story that we find an intense awareness of human loneliness.[7] Exploiting the short story's peculiar art, Mollie Panter-Downes gives voice to the submerged population of wartime women. She therefore urges us to rank her alongside her contemporaries, like Elizabeth Bowen, Sylvia Townsend Warner and Elizabeth Taylor, who also realised the form's potentials.

There are significant reasons for reviving these short stories sixty-odd years after they first and last appeared. They fill a gap in the corpus of a writer whose contributions to the literary and journalistic histories of the Second World War are considerable, if awaiting fuller appreciation. They are interesting historically because, being steeped in wartime England, they evoke those unheralded domestic dimensions of an era that, mercifully, this country is unlikely to experience again. Finally, and most importantly, they are a great pleasure to read.

Gregory LeStage
Oxford and New York, 1999

1 Gardner Botsford obituary of M P-D *The New Yorker* 10 February 1997
2 Linda Taylor review of *Wave Me Goodbye* ed. Anne Boston *The Sunday Times* 6 November 1988
3 Ernestine Carter 'Our Voice in New York' ibid. 18 April 1971
4 H.E. Bates *The Modern Short Story* London 1941 p. 8
5 Nicola Beauman obituary of M P-D *The Guardian* 31 January 1997
6 Anne Boston intro. to *Wave Me Goodbye* London 1988 p. 18
7 Frank O'Connor *The Lonely Voice* New York 1963 Ch. I

Letter from London

3 September 1939

⌒⋙⋘⌒

For a week, everybody in London had been saying every day that if there wasn't a war tomorrow there wouldn't be a war. Yesterday, people were saying that if there wasn't a war today it would be a bloody shame. Now that there is a war, the English, slow to start, have already in spirit started and are comfortably two laps ahead of the official war machine, which had to await the drop of somebody's handkerchief. In the general opinion, Hitler has got it coming to him.

The London crowds are cool – cooler than they were in 1914 – in spite of thundery weather which does its best to scare everybody by staging unofficial rehearsals for air raids at the end of breathlessly humid days. On the stretch of green turf by Knightsbridge Barracks, which used to be the scampering ground for the smartest terriers in London, has appeared a row of steam shovels that bite out mouthfuls of earth, hoist it aloft, and dump it into lorries; it is then carted away to fill sandbags. The eye has now become accustomed to sandbags everywhere and to the balloon barrage, the trap for enemy planes, which one morning spread over the sky like some form of silvery dermatitis. Posting a letter has acquired a new interest, too, since His Majesty's tubby scarlet pillar boxes have been done up in squares of yellow detector paint, which changes colour if there is poison gas in the air and is said to be as sensitive as a chameleon.

Gas masks have suddenly become part of everyday civilian equipment, and everybody is carrying the square cardboard cartons that look as though they might contain a pound of grapes for a sick friend. Bowlegged admirals stump jauntily up Whitehall with their gas masks slung neatly in knapsacks over their shoulders. Last night, London was completely blacked out. A few cars crawled through the streets with one headlight out and the other hooded while Londoners, suddenly become homebodies, sat under their shaded lights listening to a Beethoven Promenade concert interspersed with the calm and cultured tones of the B.B.C. telling motorists what to do during air raids and giving instructions to what the B.B.C. referred to coyly as expectant mothers with pink cards, meaning mothers who are a good deal more than expectant.

The evacuation of London, which is to be spaced over three days, began yesterday and was apparently a triumph for all concerned. At seven o'clock in the morning, all inward traffic was stopped and A.A. scouts raced through the suburbs whisking shrouds of sacking off imposing bulletin boards which informed motorists that all the principal routes out of town were one-way streets for three days. Cars poured out pretty steadily all day yesterday and today, packed with people, luggage, children's perambulators, and domestic pets, but the congestion at busy points was no worse than it is at any other time in the holiday season. The railways, whose workers had been on the verge of going out on strike when the crisis came, played their part nobly, and the London stations, accustomed to receiving trainloads of child refugees from the Third Reich, got down to the job of dispatching trainload after trainload of children the other way – this time, cheerful little cockneys who ordinarily get to the country perhaps once a year on the local church outing and could hardly believe the luck that was sending them now. Left behind, the mothers stood around rather listlessly at street corners waiting for the telegrams that were to be posted up at the various schools to tell them where their children were.

All over the country, the declaration of war has brought a new lease of life to retired army officers, who suddenly find themselves the commanders of battalions of willing ladies who have emerged from the herbaceous borders to answer the call of duty. Morris 10s, their windshields plastered with notices that they are engaged on business of the A.R.P. or W.V.S. (both volunteer services), rock down quiet country lanes propelled by firm-lipped spinsters who yesterday could hardly have said 'Boo!' to an aster.

Although the summer holiday is still on, village schools have reopened as centres where the evacuated hordes from London can be rested, sorted out, medically examined, refreshed with tea and biscuits, and distributed to their new homes. The war has brought the great unwashed right into the bosoms of the great washed; while determined ladies in white V.A.D. overalls search the mothers' heads with a knitting needle for unwelcome signs of life, the babies are dandled and patted on their often grimy napkins by other ladies, who have been told to act as hostesses and keep the guests from pining for Shoreditch. Guest rooms have been cleared of Crown Derby knickknacks and the best guest towels, and the big houses and cottages alike are trying to overcome the traditional British dislike of strangers, who may, for all they know, be parked with them for a matter of years, not weeks.

Everybody is so busy that no one has time to look up at the airplanes that pass overhead all day. Today was a day of unprecedented activity in the air. Squadrons of bombers bustled in all directions, and at midday an enormous number of vast planes, to which the knowing pointed as troop-carriers, droned overhead toward an unknown destination that was said by two sections of opinion to be (a) France and (b) Poland. On the ground, motor buses full of troops in bursting good humour tore through the villages, the men waving at the girls and howling 'Tipperary' and other ominously dated ditties, which everybody has suddenly remembered and found to be as good for a war in 1939 as they were in 1914.

London and the country are buzzing with rumours, a favourite one being that Hitler carries a gun in his pocket and means to shoot himself if things don't go too well; another school of thought favours the version that he is now insane and Göring has taken over. It is felt that Mussolini was up to no good with his scheme for holding a peace conference and spoiling what has become everybody's war. The English were a peace-loving nation up to two days ago, but now it is pretty widely felt that the sooner we really get down to the job, the better.

GOOD EVENING, MRS. CRAVEN: THE WARTIME STORIES OF MOLLIE PANTER-DOWNES

DATE WITH ROMANCE

14 October 1939

‹⟩∞∞∞⟨›

Mrs. Ramsay dressed for her lunch with Gerald Spalding in a mood of fine old nostalgia, well crusted on the top and five years in the wood. It took her some time to decide what to wear. After a good deal of thought she chose the navy alpaca suit with a crisp lingerie blouse, for that made her look very trim and she remembered Gerald had once said she seemed to go around protected by invisible cellophane. Mrs. Ramsay felt that it would be tragic for Gerald to sit in Malaya for five years thinking about a woman in London who looked as though she were protected by invisible cellophane and then be faced with someone limp as a wilted lettuce in crumpled chiffon. The hat was a bit of a problem. Used to women skulking about under double *terais*, Gerald would possibly shy back in alarm from an old love glimmering at him like a submerged oyster through layers of chenille fishnet or making an Ophelia-like entrance under a haystack of pansies. There was nothing in Mrs. Ramsay's cupboard that seemed to hit the note, so she went out early for her lunch date and picked up en route a quiet, ladylike little number with a touch of near-widowish melancholy in the veil. She also dropped in for a manicure. Gerald had always been rather foolish about her hands, she remembered.

1

At Gerald's club, the hall porter informed Mrs. Ramsay, in discreet confidential tones which made her feel like a naughty Ouida lady visiting a man's chambers, that Mr. Spalding had not yet arrived. The porter then came out from his dog kennel and smuggled her into a room full of imitation Chippendale furniture and genuine Sheraton members uneasily entertaining female period pieces to a glass of sherry. Mrs. Ramsay sat down on a brocaded sofa, and presently Gerald came hurrying in, fumbling with his gas-mask carton and looking harassed.

'I'm most awfully sorry,' he said. 'I got kept at the doctor's.'

'Gerald, *dear*,' said Mrs. Ramsay softly. She held out both her hands, which Gerald pumped up and down. 'Well, well,' he said, 'old Helen.' Mrs. Ramsay felt a slight but definite chill. Not noticing that the atmosphere of the tender moment had fallen several degrees, Gerald dropped her hands and sat down.

'What'll you have?' he asked.

Mrs. Ramsay thought she would take a glass of dry sherry. Gerald ordered a whisky-and-soda for himself. 'You get into the habit of *stengahs* in Malaya,' he said. 'Well, chin-chin.' They drank and gazed at each other, smiling. 'Old Helen,' Gerald repeated fatuously. 'This is nice.' Mrs. Ramsay noted coldly that he was a good deal yellower than he had been five years ago. 'How is old Charles?' he asked. 'And the kiddie? By Jove, she was only a spot of a thing when I was home on leave last.'

Mrs. Ramsay said that old Charles was well and that old Susan had, of course, been shipped off to relatives in

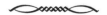

the country. 'But I don't want to talk about them, I want to talk about you,' she said. 'I want to hear all your news, Gerald.'

He patted her knee absently, as though it were the head of a retriever. 'Before we start, how about some chow?' he said.

Settled in a dim, panelled corner of the dining-room, Gerald seemed to glow richly, like some citrus fruit. His sombre eye lightened for a moment as he watched Mrs. Ramsay toying prettily with the menu. 'You've still got lovely hands, Helen,' he said, in a tone which implied that everything else had gone pretty much to rack and ruin. He ordered steamed fish and Melba toast for himself. 'I have to be careful about diet,' he said. 'It's my stomach. I told you I'd come straight from the doctor's this morning.'

Mrs. Ramsay said that she did hope it was nothing serious.

Gerald assured her, with a kind of melancholy pride, that it was. 'It's partly the East, I suppose – dysentery and all that – and partly anno Domini too, probably. We're not as young as we were, Helen.' He did some more retriever-patting under the table.

Mrs. Ramsay, wondering if the kneecap would emit a loud creak, said fretfully that she personally felt very well.

'"Age cannot wither her, nor custom stale her infinite variety,"' Gerald said loyally. 'By Jove, look at that girl's hat!' He turned round to crane after an elderly colonel escorting an attractive niece to the door. Gerald said that women's hats were the craziest things he'd seen in years, but that some of

these kids could get away with it and look pretty cute. 'Now, I knew *you'd* be wearing a sensible hat,' he said. Mrs. Ramsay smiled wanly.

With difficulty escaping from Gerald's stomach, which seemed to pursue the conversation like some particularly active octopus, they chatted about theatres. Gerald said there was nothing like a good show and he hoped the London producers would carry on, as they promised, in spite of the war. He supposed that in the East he missed a good show more than anything else. Then he told about some awfully jolly theatricals someone had got up in Singapore. Towards the end of lunch he extracted a snapshot from his cigarette case and, flushing a startling shade of burnt sienna, passed it over to Mrs. Ramsay. 'What do you think of it?' he said. Mrs. Ramsay gazed thoughtfully at a toothy young woman in a bathing suit perched at the edge of a swimming-pool. 'Strictly under the punkah, we're thinking of getting married,' Gerald explained. He said that they had met on the boat coming home and that her name was Monica. 'Of course, she's heard everything about you,' he said. '"You'll love old Helen," I told her. She's only a kid, really. Her husband was a brute – used to come home from the club stinking and knock her about in front of the servants and all that.'

Mrs. Ramsay reflected that his aim must have been indifferent, for Monica's front teeth seemed many more than were strictly usual. She passed the snapshot back to Gerald and said briskly that she was so glad.

'In spite of all she's been through, she's the youngest thing you ever saw,' said Gerald.

'Isn't that nice?' said Mrs. Ramsay. She felt that age had withered and custom staled Gerald's infinite variety considerably, and she improvised an early appointment at the hairdresser's.

'Monica can sit on her hair,' said Gerald. 'You never saw such stuff – naturally blond, too.'

Mrs. Ramsay, deciding that she would find no difficulty in sitting on Monica's hair either if Monica's head were included, said that she really must be running along now.

At the last moment, Gerald seemed inclined to be sentimental. 'I want you to meet Monica soon,' he said. 'Do you know what attracted me about her first, Helen? She reminded me of you.'

As soon as she was out of sight round the corner, Mrs. Ramsay took out her handbag mirror and anxiously inspected her teeth. They seemed much as usual and more or less under control. For a while she felt a little low; then, as she crossed the street, she caught sight of her reflection in a shop window and she couldn't help observing how nice she looked in the navy alpaca suit. It was odd how Gerald had changed when she herself looked precisely the way she had always looked. Poor Gerald, thought Mrs. Ramsay. Already she felt a good deal better as she stepped along jauntily, protected by invisible cellophane, away from the dear and mercifully stone-dead past.

MEETING AT THE PRINGLES'

6 January 1940

The committee met in the drawing-room at Laburnum Cottage, the home of two ladies invariably known as the Pringle girls. One of the Pringle girls had been wedded and widowed and was now Mrs. Carver. Neither of them was likely to see fifty again, but Pringle girls they remained, their girlishness rather ghoulishly preserved, like the dried flowers and pampas grass that rustled in the draught from the drawing-room door. The room was extremely cold. Although it was a chilly evening, there was no fire in the grate, nothing but a pyramid of more dried vegetable matter – pine cones this time, gilded and backed by a fan of pleated pink paper. It occurred to Mrs. Taylor that the committee would be a good deal cosier in the dining-room, where she had noticed the stout terrier Chappie wheezing on the rug in front of a bright little fire. Tradition, however, demanded that committees should meet in the drawing-room. Mrs. Taylor sighed, crossed her stout legs in their grey woollen stockings, and gazed expectantly at Mrs. Peake, who had risen to address the meeting.

Mrs. Peake explained that the committee had been called together to organise a Hospital Supplies Depot in the village.

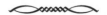

She was opening proceedings in her capacity as chairman of the local Women's Voluntary Services because *someone* had to do it – otherwise there was no reason Miss Craddock, representing the Personal Service League, or Mrs. Taylor, secretary of the Women's Institute, should not be in the chair.

'Nonsense, Doris, you do it much better,' said Miss Craddock briskly.

Mrs. Peake said she just wanted to make it clear that there were going to be no particular bosses on this job and that all the different village interests were going to pool their resources for the one cause. She would now call on Mrs. Carver to tell them more about the scheme, and, before sitting down, she would like to propose that Mrs. Carver, who had done such excellent work in the Great War, should be elected as officer-in-charge of the whole organisation.

'I second that,' snapped Miss Craddock.

Mrs. Carver said unconvincingly that it was very nice of everybody, but she didn't know why it should be her. The committee murmured polite encouragement.

'Well, if I could have Lois to help me,' Mrs. Carver said, 'I mean it's going to be quite a big job. It will take two of us easily.'

The unmarried Pringle girl, folding her arms across her thin bosom, stared gloomily at her sister through her pince-nez. 'I don't know whether I'd be much help,' she said. 'I never did have any brains, you know that, Alice.'

'Then that's carried unanimously!' Mrs. Peake cried. 'Mrs.

Carver has kindly promised to be our officer-in-charge, with Miss Lois Pringle as her second-in-command. Although this is such an informal meeting, I think someone ought to take a few notes, don't you?'

The election was duly recorded by Mrs. Taylor, and the ladies gave their attention to Mrs. Carver.

'Before we go any further, we've got to decide what work we're going to do and where we're going to do it,' Mrs. Carver announced. 'I've been to see one or two people about it already. Lois and I drove in to Sherbury this morning to see Mrs. Peters, the Regional Organiser, and I must say that what she had to say was rather upsetting. In the first place, if we want to make any surgical dressings at all, we must supply a room which can be passed as completely sterile by the medical authorities. Walls and floor washed down every time it's been used, you know, and all that nonsense. "If you insist on a room like that," I said to Mrs. Peters, "you won't get a single splint made in any village the length and breadth of England." I said to her, "In the last war my sister and I made surgical swabs by the thousand just in Mrs. Robertson's drawing-room – and there wasn't anything particularly sterile about *that*." "Well," said Mrs. Peters, "I quite see your point, Mrs. Carver, and I can't say that I'm not in sympathy with you, but those at the minute are the orders from headquarters."'

A babble of dismayed talk broke out. Everyone agreed that it was ridiculous and that there wasn't a room to meet those requirements in the village.

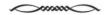

'How about the stage at the Village Hall?' suggested Mrs. Taylor. 'It's nice and bare, and I suppose we could get it scrubbed after we used it.'

'My dear, *think* of the germs in those curtains,' said Mrs. Peake, shuddering. 'All the children acting scenes from *As You Like It* and simply septic with colds and chicken pox. I really don't think it would be awfully good. How about the big playroom at the Dysons'?'

Miss Craddock reminded her that the Dysons were sleeping twenty mothers and children evacuated from London.

'There's the room at The George,' said Miss Pringle doubtfully.

'Good gracious, Lois! You don't want the dressings to reek of beer, do you?' Miss Craddock said.

'Well, if it's quite agreed that we are unable to produce a pure room in this village,' Mrs. Peake said playfully, 'I should like to say that Miss Judd has kindly offered her drawing-room and study for the use of the working party. It's got a lot to recommend it. It's central –'

'That's another thing,' said Mrs. Taylor. 'Now that we haven't got the petrol, you've got to think how people are going to get in to the Depot.'

Mrs. Peake said that they would have to consider the practicality of having one central Depot and one or two lesser ones in different parts of the village. Lady Buxton had rung her up yesterday and asked if they would like her to start a small working party at Croom, just for tenants' wives and people around. Mrs. Peake had explained that of course

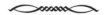

such a party would have to be affiliated as an offshoot of Mrs. Carver's, and that if Mrs. Carver had no objection –

'Not in the least,' said Mrs. Carver. 'Let her have an offshoot by all means. Let's hear more about Miss Judd's drawing-room. I can't remember if it's got cupboards or not. In the last war we used to put the work away in cardboard boxes, but in this war I suppose we'll have to be a good deal more fussy.'

After some discussion, Mrs. Taylor was able to record a resolution that it was decided to accept Miss Judd's kind offer of rooms for the working party.

'I think we'll have to start a little subscription for lighting and heating,' said Mrs. Peake.

'Yes, we'll have to have some sort of heating,' agreed Mrs. Carver.

The committee politely hid their lavender knuckles and agreed.

'It's wonderful, though, how the dahlias kept on,' said Mrs. Taylor. 'They were a sight this year. Our Jane Cowls are really a picture, only we find them a little difficult to keep from year to year – I don't know why.'

Mrs. Taylor was led back sternly from tubers to pneumonia jackets by Mrs. Carver, who said that she would write up to the Red Cross for patterns. At first, she supposed, they had better concentrate on such surgical supplies as they would be allowed to make in the septic surroundings of Miss Judd's drawing-room. She put her glasses in their case and snapped it shut, as though the Regional Organiser's neck were inside it.

11

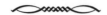

Mrs. Peake, gathering the meeting together with a smiling glance, said, 'If no other lady has any more questions to ask, I almost think we might adjourn.'

No other lady had. The committee started getting to their feet and inserting their lifeless hands into doeskin gloves. The Pringle girls came to the front door and waved goodbye, first to Miss Craddock, who got on her bicycle and shot off into the twilight, then to Mrs. Peake and Mrs. Taylor, who were going in Mrs. Peake's car. At the bow window in the dining-room, the figure of the Pringles' little maid could be seen, mounted on a carved Ashanti stool and struggling wildly among the folds of black rep with which she was completing the Laburnum Cottage blackout.

'Then I'll ring up Lady Buxton tonight about her offshoot!' shouted Mrs. Carver.

'Do!' cried Mrs. Peake. 'I know she'll be helpful.'

The ladies drove away and the Pringle girls went indoors to sit by the dining-room fire with Chappie and the wireless. They had missed the six o'clock news, but at nine o'clock the familiar gentlemanly voice told bits about the war and the King and ration cards. After it was over, Mrs. Carver went out into the hall to telephone Lady Buxton. Lois could hear her voice, brisk and cheerful, in the pauses between 'Tipperary' and other jolly old favourites that the B.B.C. was relaying from a soldiers' concert party.

'It's a long way to Tipperar-ee –'

'Of course it's nonsense!' Mrs. Carver was shouting into the telephone. 'I said to Mrs. Peters that you'd never find a

perfectly antiseptic room in any village. "In the last war," I said to her –'

'But my heart's right there!' roared the voices of the potential customers in whose service the ladies were being so busy and happy – happier, as a matter of fact, than they had been for the last twenty-one years.

MRS. RAMSAY'S WAR

27 January 1940

It was before lunch on a dark January day in the Ramsays' country cottage in Sussex. Just how dark January could be, Mrs. Ramsay reflected gloomily, no one would ever know who had not spent it in a delightful little Tudor gem with a wealth of old oak and several interesting original features (such as the beam on which you knocked your head outside the bathroom). The log fire was smoking in its interesting original way and an angry hiss of plumbing told the exact whereabouts of Nannie Hunter and her charge. Mrs. Ramsay was brooding over the tendency of these fascinating old houses to filter noise upwards and downward when the door opened and Mrs. Parmenter came in, carrying a bunch of snowdrops in one hand and a small vase in the other.

'I just had to run out between the showers and get a few,' she said. 'A room never looks like home without flowers, don't you agree, dear?'

Mrs. Ramsay thought it would take the Chelsea Flower Show to make this one feel like home but that perhaps it was beginning to feel like Mrs. Parmenter's home. Mrs. Parmenter was Alison Hunter's mother, a widow who lived in a handsome flat in Prince's Gate. When war broke out, Mrs.

Hunter had rung up and asked if Mrs. Ramsay would have her little girl and Nannie to stay for the duration down at the Sussex cottage. Mrs. Hunter herself was driving an ambulance and couldn't leave town.

'Camilla will be nice company for your Susan,' she had said.

Mrs. Ramsay mentioned mildly that Alan Carpenter and his nurse were staying there too, so Susan would have quite a party. Mrs. Hunter then asked if Mrs. Ramsay could possibly have Mrs. Parmenter – for a bit, anyway. Mrs. Ramsay had replied firmly that she couldn't possibly do it, but Mrs. Hunter had said that Mummy would be no trouble because she would bring Jessie to help in the house, and that the whole party would arrive on Tuesday.

'You've taken *such* a load off my mind, Helen darling,' she had said, ringing off, and on Tuesday the load had arrived as advertised, in a hired Daimler which bulged with Mrs. Parmenter, Camilla on Nannie's knee, several rolls of bedding, the parlourmaid, two Pekinese, and a quantity of luggage.

All autumn Mrs. Parmenter had run out between the showers and picked the asters, saying brightly that an old woman must be allowed to do something around the house. Opposition would hardly have been hysterical if she had offered to make the beds, but her tastes appeared to be floral. Now it was January and the snowdrops, and before you knew where you were, Mrs. Ramsay thought morbidly, it would be May and the tulips. Somehow she had never expected to spend the war having a Battle of Flowers with Mrs. Parmenter.

'Such a nasty day,' said Mrs. Parmenter, standing off from the vase to see the effect. 'San Toy has got his asthma again, poor little dog.'

Mrs. Ramsay said quickly that she was afraid the cottage was damp and wasn't really meant for a winter home.

'But how we shall revel in the spring when it comes!' cried Mrs. Parmenter. 'There! Don't their brave little faces give you fresh hope?' Mrs. Ramsay felt that it would take more than a few snowdrops to give her fresh hope. It would take something really big, like the back end of a Daimler loaded with Parmenter luggage going rapidly towards London.

Mrs. Parmenter, abandoning the brave little faces and adopting a steelier note, asked if Yum-Yum could have less potato in his dinner today.

'I'm *afraid* your nice cookie doesn't quite understand how drefful spoilt my little fellows are,' she said.

Jessie came tripping through the hall and sounded the gong, nostalgia for Prince's Gate written large in every loop of her crisp organdie bows. She then retreated into the dining-room, and a confused roaring noise announced that the children were coming downstairs for the communal nursery lunch. Everyone got wedged into the room somehow, bibs were hitched round necks, and a subterranean wheezing located Mrs. Parmenter's little fellows right under their patron's chair. Mrs. Ramsay, carving the lamb and listening to the nurses babbling of cardigan patterns, thought moodily that this kind of thing might go on for years. Of course it would be fascinating to watch the children growing up right

under one's eyes. The girls would become young women almost imperceptibly and Mrs. Parmenter would be running out between the showers to pick the roses for Camilla's wedding bouquet.

Mrs. Parmenter was asking if she had heard from Charles. 'It must be such a comfort to you, dear, to know that he's safe, at any rate,' she said, 'and such a comfort to him to feel that *you're* being well looked after.' Her roguish eye implied that without her restraining chaperonage Mrs. Ramsay would be helling around Sussex, probably in the nude.

Mrs. Ramsay, smiling wanly, said that she didn't know if an anti-aircraft gun near an arsenal was so terribly safe, really, but Mrs. Parmenter said that she'd heard on good authority that the Germans were not going to send over many raids. 'This came straight from Winnie Carruthers, whose nephew is something very high up in the War Office, so I think we can rely on it,' she said.

Mrs. Ramsay resisted the impulse to ask why, if Winnie Carruthers' nephew was as reliable as all that, Mrs. Parmenter and Jessie were not sitting cosily in Prince's Gate. All the children ate very slowly, apparently acting on the Gladstonian principle of thorough mastication. Their nurses urged them on, still chattering of cardigans.

'What is it, Jessie?' asked Mrs. Parmenter, inspecting the steamed apple pudding, which Jessie proffered, as though it were straight from the recipe book of the Borgias. Then she said that if Mrs. Ramsay's nice cookie wouldn't be offended, she would just take a little fresh fruit.

After lunch the nurses, hung round with gas masks, took the children for a walk. Mrs. Ramsay wanted to write to Charles, but Mrs. Parmenter was at the writing table, so she went out to find the gardener, a dour and hairy man who seldom if ever talked of cardigans. He said nothing about revelling in the spring but prophesied the failure of all the early crops and aimed a clod of earth at one of Mrs. Parmenter's little fellows who was delicately scratching in the onion bed. Mrs. Ramsay found him a great comfort. When she got back to the house, Mrs. Parmenter was still at the writing table.

That evening Susan, saying good night, remarked that she didn't want Camilla and Alan to go, ever. Mrs. Ramsay felt impelled to hit her smartly over the head but instead went downstairs to the living-room, where Mrs. Parmenter was knitting under the good light and listening to the wireless.

'I was just thinking, dear, that if you had no objection I might get a few of my own things down from Prince's Gate,' she said. 'One does miss one's own bits and pieces, don't you agree?'

Mrs. Ramsay, picking her way among suspiciously growling Pekinese, remembered with a good deal of wistfulness the poet's assurance that the grave was a fine and private place.

After the nine o'clock news bulletin, Mrs. Parmenter let Yum-Yum and San Toy into the garden, where they disappeared in a frenzy of yapping. 'They feel they're

guarding me,' said Mrs. Parmenter indulgently. 'Silly little Yum-Yum, don't you know that it's not *our* home, sweetheart?'

Mrs. Ramsay felt that it was, though.

IN CLOVER

13 April 1940

~∞~

At the time the London *évacués* had come to the village, Miss Vereker, the billeting officer, had looked up from her list and said to Mrs. Clark, '*You're* going to be lucky. You're going to Mrs. Fletcher at the Manor.' She had smiled as she spoke, the flashing and more than necessarily kind smile that she reserved for the lower orders, who hadn't, don't you know, had quite the advantages that we have.

None of the Clarks had smiled back at the chintzy lady in the broad hat, sitting with pencil poised as though she were making out a bulb order. Dazed, poor creatures, by the journey, Miss Vereker decided. The baby, sitting impassively in its mother's arms, wore a dirty red knitted cap in which it oddly resembled a wizened old sans-culotte, a mummified Marat with a snotty nose. It was overpoweringly evident that Mrs. Clark was again – expectant, Miss Vereker delicately phrased it to herself, without noticing that the word didn't fit in very well with Mrs. Clark's air of dully awaiting a blow over the head with a blunt instrument. She said quickly, 'I do hope they've given you a nice cup of tea. A cup of tea does so pull one together, don't you think?' Mrs. Clark said hoarsely that she'd had one, and Miss Vereker remembered having observed the

21

party being refreshed across the room, the infant Marat taking a swig from the saucer. So there was nothing to do but give the woman and her three children their labels and send them up to the manor in charge of one of the Girl Guides. Watching the party trail to the door, she wondered doubtfully if dear little Mrs. Fletcher really had known what she was letting herself in for when she volunteered to take in a few of the London *évacués*.

Little Mrs. Fletcher, it turned out, hadn't an idea. She had two babies of her own and a husband in the Guards, but her notions about all three were pretty innocent. On the afternoon her nurse went out, the harsher facts of infant life were concealed from her by the nursery maid, who let her have fun pretending to fool around with two little dears who were always perfectly dry, perfectly sweet-smelling, and done up in frilly organdie tied with ribbons. Her first sight of the dreadful Clark baby shook her a good deal. It was the same with pregnancy, which she associated with chaise-longues, dreamy meanderings through layette catalogues, and 'cloud' dinner dresses that were supposed to blur the unromantic aspects of the affair in layers of chiffon. There was something about the straining third button of Mrs. Clark's jacket that upset Mrs. Fletcher. Of course, she was perfectly sensible about it. She had known that her guests were coming from one of the poorest parts of London and it was natural they should look dingy, but she had imagined a medium dinginess that would wear off with one or two good scrubbings and a generous handout of gingham pinafores. The dinginess of

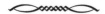

the Clarks, which seemed to have soaked in far deeper than just their skins, was a setback, but Mrs. Fletcher met it with her most charming smile. She even drew one of the children towards her as she talked, and stood with an arm round his bony shoulders, trying not to shudder, thinking that she must take a good hot bath before she went anywhere near the nursery.

'I do hope you'll be comfortable,' she said to Mrs. Clark. 'It used to be the chauffeur's flat until he moved into a cottage. There's a nice bathroom and a little kitchen, and a gas ring in the sitting room that will come in handy for heating up your baby's bottles and things.' Then, flustered by the silent, staring Clarks, she cried, 'And now I know what you'd like! You'd like a nice cup of tea.'

The Clarks heard her without surprise. By now they were used to smiling ladies, old or young, who urged them distractedly to have a nice cup of tea.

Mrs. Fletcher was sensible about the various other setbacks that she encountered in the following weeks. When the young Clarks proved to be no more house-trained than the six-week-old poodle puppy her husband had given her for her birthday, Mrs. Fletcher went up to town in the Rolls and ordered two or three new mattresses and another bale of fleecy peach-coloured blankets; it was really as simple as that. Something told her that none of the servants would welcome the idea of going over and cleaning up for Mrs. Clark, who was obviously incapable of cleaning up for herself, so Mrs. Fletcher hired a village woman, who came up and indignantly shook out mops and flung open windows for an hour every morning. Even this lady's activities were unable to get the smell out of the place. There didn't seem to be a disinfectant invented that could drown the Clark smell of grinding, abject poverty, very different from the decent, cottage variety with a red geranium on the window sill, which had been the worst Mrs. Fletcher had encountered up to now.

As the weeks went by, the Clarks began to get her down. In spite of the war, in spite of all the terrible things that were happening in Europe, there were still things Mrs. Fletcher would have been unable to help enjoying – simple things, like fine mornings, and the colours the trees were turning, and crumpets for tea by the fire with the dogs attentive and the children being brought down afterwards in their best smocks. Her husband was away, but then all the husbands were away. The old butler was the only man in the house, but flowers were sent in regularly from the greenhouses, her breakfast coffee tasted the same; she was twenty-four years old, in splendid health, and it would have been impossible not to laugh now and then, even though the radio in the library kept on saying those dreadful things. If it hadn't been for the Clarks.

That rickety little procession, staggering on mean legs across the pattern of Mrs. Fletcher's day, seemed like the first warning crack in the safe, dependable fabric of existence. Everything was the same, and yet it wasn't the same. Perhaps it never would be again. She would wake in the night and start thinking about the Clarks, and the next morning she would drop in at the chauffeur's flat to have a cosy, woman-to-woman chat with Mrs. Clark. It never worked out well, though. Mrs. Fletcher tried to talk to Mrs. Clark as she would have talked to any young mother, but it was difficult to think of this flabby creature with the shocking teeth as a young mother. The horrifying notion made Mrs. Fletcher's ears turn rosy among her foxes as she fumbled through her attempts at interplanetary communication, the children standing round her chair, their heads too large and wise above their pot-bellied bodies.

'I do *hope* you'll tell me if there's anything you want,' she would say earnestly, hopeful that it might all simplify down to something which could be settled by the stroke of a pen on a cheque.

At Christmas, the father came to see them. Mrs. Fletcher's husband was home, too. 'My God, what a specimen!' Captain Fletcher said as they passed the Clarks in the lime avenue, Mr. Clark trundling the infant Marat in a push-chair. Mrs. Fletcher sighed. Mr. Clark's cough floated back to them, resigned and dispirited, like the droop of the shoulders under his shabby coat.

'How are they going to bear it when the war's over and they have to go back?' she said.

'Time enough to start worrying about that when the war's over,' her husband suggested comfortably.

The war was still going on, however, the morning Miss Vereker, summoned by telephone, pedalled up the lime avenue on her bicycle, bending her head to keep the spring rain out of her eyes. Poor little Mrs. Fletcher, she thought.

It really was too bad. She could hardly wait to give up her Burberry and rubbers to the butler before darting in to tell Mrs. Fletcher how bad it was.

'Taking those poor children back to London just as the air raids may be going to start! And in her condition, with everything so *imminent*, don't you know.' Mrs. Fletcher was still at breakfast; Miss Vereker refused coffee abstractedly. 'It's really too disheartening, my dear, after all you did for them.'

'I thought that they'd settled down. They seemed to be comfortable,' Mrs. Fletcher said helplessly.

'Comfortable? Why, they were in clover!' cried Miss Vereker. 'Did the woman give any reason for going, or did she simply walk out on you?'

Mrs. Fletcher crumbled a curl of Melba toast. 'No, she gave a reason. She said that she couldn't be away from her husband any more. She just wanted to go home.'

Mrs. Fletcher looked flushed and astonished, almost as though she was going to cry. There were various other details to discuss, for after the Clarks had gone it turned out that the chauffeur's quarters weren't in a very nice condition. It was probably best to be on the safe side and burn nearly everything.

'The expense those ungrateful wretches have put you to!' Miss Vereker said.

Mrs. Fletcher only wished the rest of the Clark episode could be disposed of so easily. She had a dreadful feeling that something of the Clarks would be there for keeps, making her uncertain, making her believe what the library radio would

tell her, even though her breakfast coffee smelled good in its spode cup and the young gardener, kneeling out in the hall with his back to her, was cunningly hiding the ugly freesia pots in a good, deep layer of moss.

IT'S THE REAL THING THIS TIME

15 June 1940

Major Marriot lived with his unmarried sister in a charming cottage, one of the hundreds all over England which, built for the British workingman, are ending their days in gentility as homes for the poor but snug gentry. Chintzes fluttered at its doll windows and a pretty card, hand-painted by Miss Marriot, warned 'Heads!' above the lopsided front door, which usually stood ajar and treated passers-by to a glimpse of an arsenal of Zulu shields, bows, and assagais. The Major, who was a tall man, a grizzled Adonis with a bristling cavalry moustache and a complexion midway between strong Ceylon tea and pigskin, somehow contrived to maintain his erect military bearing, although most of his waking hours were spent in a crouching position, either dodging beams indoors or squatting in the garden weeding. Both he and his sister were fervent gardeners. Little Mrs. Trent, whose husband was in France and who often felt lonely, knew she could find them working on most fine days, the Major busy among the vegetables, Miss Marriot tying up the clematis and wearing a dress so flowery that many foiled bees buzzed angrily round her for a moment before going on to the less deceiving columbines.

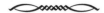

'Come in and have a glass of sherry,' Miss Marriot would cry through a mouthful of raffia. 'You're just in time for the six o'clock news. Gerald! Here is Mrs. Trent!'

The Major was always ready to leave the lettuces and come and twinkle gallantly at a pretty face. He had a soft corner in his heart for Mrs. Trent. Once, when she told him she had heard from her husband the day before but that there hadn't been any real news about the war because they weren't, of course, allowed to say much, his small, bloodshot eyes rested on her tenderly and he groaned, 'There never is any real news. They aren't goin' to tell us anything. Did you hear the guns this morning?' Mrs. Trent said yes, she had heard them. 'Just practice firin',' said the Major, mournfully. 'For a moment I thought it might be the real thing,' and he glanced wistfully into the hall, where Mrs. Trent knew that all the paraphernalia of an air-raid warden was laid out on a small table under the assagais. The various pieces of equipment were arranged as neatly as though they were silver bric-a-brac – a whistle, a hand rattle, packets of field dressings, bleach paste for gas casualties, and a large bell which the Major was going to brandish somehow in the intervals between rattling and whistling. Occasionally, Mrs. Trent had seen the Major pick up the rattle, look at it longingly, and put it down again, like a small boy with a parcel which he knows he mustn't open till Christmas.

One evening shortly after the fighting started in Norway, Mrs. Trent went indoors with the Marriots to listen to their radio and drink their sherry. The Major liked the radio turned up so loud that the glossy pink cheeks of Miss

Marriot's Staffordshire figures seemed to wobble on their shuddering bracket. A portrait of some military ancestor in a red coat had been removed to make room for an enormous map of Scandinavia, into which the Major ferociously jabbed flags on pins as he shouted at the radio, 'Turn their flank, you fools!' and 'That's what you get for mechanisin' all the cavalry!' The cottage smelled of furniture cream, lavender in bowls, and of the vegetable curry that the maid was preparing for the evening meal – fiery-hot to please the Major's palate, full of vitamins for Miss Marriot. Sipping his whisky-and-water, the Major said gloomily, 'If only they'd ask me, I could tell 'em something. But when those fellas at the War House put you on the shelf –' and he got up to lunge a flag into the map as though he wished it were an assagai between German shoulder blades.

Mrs. Trent knew, of course, how he had offered his services to the country in the early days of the war. She had seen him setting off for the station, debonair in his town clothes and spats, with a late rosebud in his buttonhole. 'Just runnin' up to have a chat with someone at the War House!' he had shouted over the hedge, not forgetting to shoot her the tender, killing glance which made her see what a charmer he must have been, even after that polo pony broke his nose and the Afghan bullet took a nick out of one eyebrow. It was all very painful when he walked the spaniel along to her house and dropped in for a drink late that evening. He was drooping like the rosebud that was still in his buttonhole, and she had to be very fluttering and helpless, to be a silly little woman over finding the whisky decanter and mixing his

nasty man's drink, before he bucked up and told her, with a charming, naïve conceit, how surprised the fellas at the War House had been when they learned his real age. 'I fancy they'd placed me a good ten years younger,' he said with a chuckle; it had been no good, they had told him politely they didn't want him. 'Just a dugout,' he said, making a joke of it, and sat looking like the spaniel, jowly and mournful, staring with red, blinking eyes out at the English elms that refused to turn into French poplars, the evening sky in which there was a star but never a Very light.

When Germany invaded Holland and Belgium, the tallboy and a couple of sporting prints had to be shifted to make room for another tremendous map, over which the Major brooded lovingly, whistling through his teeth. 'It's beginnin' at last, 'pon my soul it is,' he said. 'Yes, we're in it now, every man, woman, and child of us.' He took a cigarette and fitted it into his long ivory holder, smiling dreamily to himself. His eyes were very bright. 'Yes, it's the real thing this time,' he said happily. Mrs. Trent didn't see him or Miss Marriot for the next day or two, so she didn't know whether he had gone up to town again to interview the War Office. Then one evening she took the dogs for a run past the Marriots' cottage. The windows were already blacked out, and she was somewhat startled to see a figure standing motionless in the twilight under the apple trees. It turned out to be the Major, staring intently upwards and nursing a gun. He was keepin' a sharp lookout, he explained, at dawn and dusk, as the authorities had requested. 'They dropped the poor devils by parachute

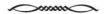

in Holland. I shouldn't be a bit surprised if that fella was mad enough to try it here,' he said hopefully.

He shifted the gun from one arm to the other and looked up again at the sky. Mrs. Trent could see in the half-light that he was smiling sweetly as he sometimes smiled at her, with the rakish twinkle of the born charmer, the absent-minded tenderness of a man who loved women and danger but had somehow ended up with Miss Marriot and a warden's rattle beneath crossed assagais. The Major looked up for the falling body of a German soldier like a lover watching for a sign from a stubbornly closed window.

'Yes, I shouldn't be surprised if we aren't in for a packet of trouble,' he said.

THIS FLOWER, SAFETY

6 July 1940

⌒⟩⟨⌒

Miss Mildred Ewing had lived at the Hotel San Remo, Crumpington-on-Sea, since the beginning of the war. Her London house, one of those vast, dirty stucco fortresses of the past that are still to be seen in the squares of Belgravia, was untenanted except for an old caretaker living in the basement. Although the rooms had been put away carefully under dust sheets, their contents packed in newspapers or tenderly wrapped in baize, the dust had probably seeped in to lie in the dulling mahogany curlicues of the Chippendale chairs, the Georgian silver must be tarnishing slowly, the china cupids acquiring a film of grey on their dimpled pink thighs. Miss Ewing thought of this gradual disintegration of her property with calm, even with indifference. Before the war cut her life so sharply in two, she had cherished her possessions jealously. The best of the silver had mounted to bed with the butler every night; rather than risk the slapdash methods of the modern housemaid, Miss Ewing had washed the china cupids herself, with her sleeves rolled high on her thin arms and her diamond rings in a little pile beside the basin. Now that she had discovered the important truth that her flesh was as brittle as theirs and far more precious, the safety of china cupids had become irrelevant.

35

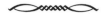

Miss Ewing was safe at Crumpington-on-Sea. She and her elderly maid, Sparks, enjoyed the security of that sunny little watering place, which was sometimes quite like the Riviera, really. Sparks enjoyed it a good deal more than the previous annual sojourns in Nice or Mentone. What with the library and a couple of cinemas and the Crumpington Pavilion, where a women's orchestra played jolly operatic selections at teatime, Sparks found plenty of entertainment for every minute of the day, and it was nice not to have people speaking a foreign lingo round you. She quickly found cronies, too, for there were other elderly ladies with maids staying at the San Remo. At dinner, the white heads made the dining-room look like a cotton field at harvest; if the war news was 'upsetting', they became tremulous and the diamond earrings bobbed and quivered in the frail old ears. Miss Ewing and the other ladies dreaded bad news, because it reacted distressingly on their digestive system, causing quite a run on sodamints at the chemist's and a constant pattering of feet in the upper corridors of the hotel during the small hours of the morning. On the whole, however, the war seemed reassuringly remote from this cheerful haven – from the attentive headwaiter respectfully suggesting a nice Graves and the Crumpington Pavilion ladies merrily scraping away at *Carmen*. Everyone said that Crumpington-on-Sea was the safest place in England. One spring day, Mrs. Prentiss received a letter which she read aloud in the lounge. The letter was from her son, who was something high up in the War Office, and it said what a great relief it was to feel that Mrs. Prentiss was there, well out of the way of air raids. Hearing high authority's assurance that they

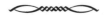

had picked a good spot, Miss Ewing and the other ladies nodded at each other pleasantly over their knitting; all the teagown laps were full of khaki and navy-blue wool that would end up as comforts for the brave boys who were having such a horrid time somewhere so that the Graves could arrive properly chilled on Miss Ewing's table and Mrs. Prentiss could be lugged in a Bath chair unmolested along the sea front.

'Oh, yes, we're wonderfully safe here,' said Miss Challoner, shooing her fox terrier off a completed Balaclava. 'If you come to think of it, there's nothing near that could possibly interest the Germans – not an aerodrome or a camp or anything.'

The ladies thought of it, and agreed with Miss Challoner that Crumpington did seem to be especially blessed. That night, as she was putting her mistress to bed, Sparks suggested that Miss Ewing might write to the London caretaker and arrange for the most valuable china and silver to be removed to the bank.

'I don't care what happens to it,' said Miss Ewing. 'I don't care if I never see it again. Probably I shan't go back to London when the war is over.'

'Oh now, Madam, you'd think very different if it was the season starting, and all your friends there, and the opera coming on and all,' Sparks said, tucking in the eiderdown.

'No, I shall never go back,' said Miss Ewing, thinking with a shudder of those dreadfully 'upsetting' last days, of the sirens sounding, of people running in the square, their gas masks thumping against their backs. When Sparks thought

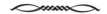

of London, she saw Miss Ewing in her sables setting off for Covent Garden. When Miss Ewing thought of London, she saw herself lying dead in the wreckage of her father's Chippendale dining suite, the dust drifting down on her upturned face.

'Mrs. Prentiss's son says that we're so safe here,' she said.

'Yes, we're in the best place, no doubt, Madam,' said Sparks. 'Though it doesn't seem that there's going to be any real war, not what you might call war, does it?'

Feeling pleasantly drowsy, Miss Ewing murmured, 'Miss Challoner thinks there's bound to be a revolution in Germany soon. She's always so well-informed. Pull the curtains right back when you've put the light out, Sparks. I like to hear the sea.'

It was a shock when, only a day or two later, things began to happen. One morning, before the old ladies had got their teeth in or their curled fronts adjusted or their stays laced for the day, the terrible noise started. The China tea slopped over in the trembling saucer as Miss Ewing listened, the windows in the Palm Court shivered as though gripped by an ague. At lunchtime nobody could eat, everyone was listening for the next heart-stopping rumble of gunfire. That night there were several muffled explosions that the headwaiter, not so attentive over the wine list as usual, thought might be depth charges out in the Channel.

Later, Sparks, peeping cautiously through the bedroom curtains, reported big flashes from the sea. 'It's a raid going on over there, I should say, Madam,' she said. She looked

mysteriously flushed and exhilarated, something like an elderly vivandière as she clutched the bottle of brandy that Miss Ewing always had, in case of emergencies, beside her bed.

'Put down the brandy and go to bed,' Miss Ewing commanded her sharply.

Miss Ewing had a shocking night and came down next morning, grey-faced, to find that one or two of the more nervous hotel guests had already left. The gunfire rumbled away across the Channel all that week, sometimes louder, sometimes softer. A picture fell off the wall in Miss Challoner's room, narrowly missing the fox terrier, and Mrs. Prentiss's son wrote that it might be as well if his mother tried a change, say to Torquay, for a bit. After she had gone the rout set in. The lift made innumerable wheezing journeys up and down, packed with suitcases. Hired Daimlers stood at the door, and the old ladies stepped in, followed by maids with rugs and jewel cases, and sped away, part of the tragic pattern of speeding cars, trudging people, laden farm carts, that was spreading out over the face of Europe. Miss Ewing went, too, having wired to a married nephew who lived in the depths of the country, far removed from the coast, to expect her and Sparks for a visit.

Miss Ewing arrived at her nephew's old house and was comforted because it was set so deeply in leafy lanes. For the first few days she did nothing but sit about listening to the silence, drinking it in greedily, as though it were a precious draught of spring water. Planes passed overhead a good deal,

but she was quickly able to distinguish the red, white, and blue circles, and after a bit they gave her a comfortable feeling of security, like the sight of a policeman going the rounds at night. With a little imagination, it would almost have been possible to forget the war completely. Of course, there was the wireless, but she avoided listening to it as much as possible. Her nephew and his wife listened at all hours; their eldest boy had got his commission in October. Miss Ewing sat out in the garden and knitted him a Balaclava. Her appetite was marvellous. During those terrible last days at Crumpington she had been unable to eat anything, but now she ate an excellent dinner, slept like a top, and woke up looking forward to the weighty breakfast tray with which Sparks staggered upstairs every morning.

'We're so safe here, Sparks. We ought to be very grateful,' she said, pouring out her coffee and just glancing quickly at the headlines of the nice little picture paper, which made everything sound so much better than *The Times* did. Sparks, who hankered after the fleshpots of Crumpington, agreed somewhat sourly.

One night, a week or so after Miss Ewing's arrival, her nephew and his wife discussed in low tones the possibility of Aunt Mildred's leaving, and decided hopelessly that she was there for the duration. Fate, however, arranged otherwise. A couple of nights later a lone German bomber, making off in a hurry after an unsuccessful search for the flying field from which Miss Ewing's friendly red, white, and blue planes came, unloaded his bombs over some woods only a mile or so from the house. The noise of the explosions, followed by the sound

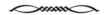

of fire engines dashing by, the local gentlemen in wardens' tin hats rushing about, the sight of Sparks shivering in the gas mask which she had donned at the first explosion all put Miss Ewing in a state of prostration which even the brandy couldn't help much. Next day a man was putting new glass in the damaged windows as Miss Ewing came downstairs, gloved and toqued, followed by Sparks, white-faced from night alarums and morning packing. While they waited for the hired car, Miss Ewing's nephew asked where she was going. The wings on her toque quivered agitatedly as she cried, 'Anywhere! Anywhere to be quiet, to be safe!' Less vaguely, she said that she was heading for a secluded hotel, high on a Welsh mountain; what seemed like a systematic German persecution could hardly follow her there.

'You'll be just in time to get a good view of the invasion from Ireland, Aunt Mildred,' her nephew said with a touch of malice.

Tugging at a doeskin glove so violently that it split at the seam, she stared at him and groaned, 'Do they really think it will come that way?'

'It's been suggested,' he said.

'Then where – *where* can one count on being safe?' cried Miss Ewing, reaching for her bag as though she had a vague idea that it might contain the note, the coin, with which to purchase this urgent necessity.

'Nowhere,' he said sombrely.

At that moment the car appeared and Miss Ewing, getting in, sped away once more with her maid, her jewel case, her travelling rugs – the sad little caravan which was all that

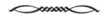

remained of her treasure on earth. If necessary for her safety, she would jettison even those remnants as ruthlessly as the German pilot had jettisoned his bombs. To be safe, that was all that mattered – to die in her own time and her own bed and not be splattered with anonymous violence over some stranger's field. 'It's such a quiet hotel, right up on that mountain,' she said to the silent Sparks. 'Nothing like the San Remo, of course, but it's well out of the way of things. There's nothing round there that could possibly attract – you know what.' After a pause she added loudly, defiantly, as though someone had spoken, 'Nothing!' and dabbed her handkerchief against her unsteady lips.

AS THE FRUITFUL VINE

31 August 1940

‿⸝⸝⸝⸝‿

Lucy Grant had to admit that none of the big moments of her life had really come up to expectations. Something had always missed fire somewhere. When she thought back to all the memorable occasions of her twenty-five years, they greeted her with the identical damp, depressing fizzle of squibs which hadn't performed quite according to schedule. Her childhood was littered with these disappointments, her adolescence offered example after example of the budding and wilting of bright hopes. There had been the time, for instance, of her graduation from Oxford with honours, a proud moment entirely overshadowed by her elder sister's engagement to a more than satisfactory suitor. It was amazing how often Valerie had been responsible for the damping and wilting process. Of course, it couldn't be said that she had anything to do with directing the limelight away from Lucy at Lucy's own wedding. That was the fault of the war, which made it necessary for her and Philip Grant to get married quietly during one of his hurried leaves, without any of the trimmings of gold braid, crossed swords, fluttering brides-maids, and admiring friends to which she had looked forward. Although naturally she was blissfully happy, she couldn't help being a little regretful.

After a few days' honeymoon, Philip had to rejoin his ship, and it was with the greatest astonishment that Lucy discovered in due course that she was going to have a baby. It seemed less like a marital than a botanical incident, the result of a chance brush between a bee and a flower. This discovery of motherhood ought to have been stirring, but again a big moment didn't quite come off. Paternity would catch up with Philip somewhere in the West Indies or the Mediterranean or wherever Lucy's startled letter reached him; his reply would reach her long after any emotions which she might have been feeling at the moment of writing his letter had passed. To be truthful, those emotions were not overpowering. It was difficult to work up emotion over a tender secret which had to be shouted to a bee who was now winging his way God knows where. Once more, Lucy felt, life had treated her cruelly.

The way in which her family received the news was also as she might have expected. Her parents, instead of raising an excited to-do about the first grandchild, did not try to hide the fact that they considered 1940 an inauspicious year for babies. 'You might,' said her mother reproachfully, 'have waited.' Lucy had imagined her weeping a little and immediately setting to work on something complicated in fuzzy pink Angora, but both these impulses were out of date in a world where the bombs were already dropping fast. In her mother's day a pregnant woman spent a good deal of time on a sofa, thinking beautiful thoughts and resolutely avoiding unpleasant ones; people took care not to speak of anything shocking or violent in front of her. Nowadays shocking things

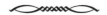

turned up on the doorstep with the morning paper; violence was likely to crash out of a summer sky on a woman who could move only slowly and who was not as spry as usual at throwing herself on her face in the gutter. Belatedly, Lucy's mother explained, 'Of course, I'm glad, darling. It's only that I wish you'd chosen a happier time – you and Philip.' The anxious lines settling deeper round her eyes, she said, 'I'm sure Philip would want you to be very careful, Lucy dear. Don't bother to read too many papers, and don't listen to that horrible wireless more than you need. All you've got to think about from now on is keeping well and cheerful and having a healthy, beautiful baby.' It seemed only a step from there to a few cosy tears and a chat about pink Angora, but her courageous Coué* broke down miserably. 'Daddy and I think that you'd better move out of that flat,' she said. 'It's got no air-raid shelter at all.' Her worried eyes told Lucy that she didn't really believe all that smooth stuff about having a healthy, beautiful baby. She believed only in terror and a grandson who would always be slightly queer because he was born, as people would whisper significantly, during one of the worst air bombardments of the war.

Lucy found that her friends reacted to the news in the same way. Women's eyes had a habit of sliding past her with a clairvoyant look; in that brief, unguarded second between

* A nineteenth-century French pharmacist who developed a form of psychotherapy dependent on auto-suggestion. The key phrase of his system was: 'Every day, and in every way, I am becoming better and better.'

smiles her friends listened only too plainly to ghostly bombs crashing. Although she was feeling remarkably well, their manner assumed that she was a stretcher case already. She had hoped to have fun discussing layettes and possible names, but so far as she could see, the spectacle of an expectant young mother with a gas mask thumping against her ribs turned the thoughts of observers to deep shelters rather than to organdie. Aunts who had always been fonder of Valerie now kissed Lucy with mournful affection and asked her to stay with them in the country. 'London at this time of year is so hot and dusty,' they put it delicately. Lucy began to feel like a housemaid who had gone wrong and was being treated with inflexible kindness by some charitable organisation. After she gave up the flat and moved home, to please her mother, there was a conspiracy to keep any news of naval losses from her, since the clairvoyant friends knew that something was bound to happen to Philip. She arrived home one afternoon to find her mother, white and tremulous, hovering over a telegram which turned out to be from a cousin who was coming up from Devonshire for the sales and wanted Lucy to meet her at a matinée. Holding the telegram, Lucy looked apologetically at her mother, who was pretending, with a touch of hysteria, that of course she had guessed it was from Monica all the time. Monica's mother was one of the aunts who had suggested that Lucy should come down and stay for a bit. 'Now, why don't you go back with Monica?' Lucy's mother said, looking at her eagerly. 'The change would do you good, darling.'

'I might,' Lucy said.

Perhaps it would be a relief to get out of London, the city in which she seemed to be the only pregnant woman. Although it was too early for any change to show in her figure, she was morbidly certain that people in the street stared at her with pity and curiosity; the manner of the shopgirl who sold her some little vests yesterday had been surely over-solicitous. At a time in her life when she might reasonably expect to feel proud and happy, she felt merely sheepish. It really was too bad.

Valerie turned up next day, looking cool and trim in her nurse's uniform. She and Bernard had given their country house to be used as a convalescent home for officers; photographs of Valerie, sitting efficiently at her desk or smiling efficiently at a convalescent major lying wrapped in rugs on the terrace, had appeared in one or two of the weeklies. Valerie had always been efficient as far back as Lucy could remember. The war was going well for her, like everything else. Bernard had an important job which kept him in London.

'For heaven's sake,' she said to Lucy, 'do go to Aunt Kitty's and stop us all having miscarriages for you every time the siren goes.'

'But it's such nonsense,' said Lucy feebly. 'I'm strong as a horse. I've never felt better.'

Valerie looked at her. 'I'll admit this business of having a baby suits you,' she said. 'You're positively blooming.'

There was something strangely grudging in her expression which made Lucy glance at her with sudden attention, and the conventional words somehow didn't sound quite right. For a moment Lucy sat perfectly still, then she asked, softly and carelessly, 'Why haven't you and Bernard ever tried it, Val? I've often wondered.'

Valerie got up and took a cigarette from the box on the table. She was rather a time lighting it and finding a place to put the match. 'Well, I don't know,' she said. 'I suppose we wanted a few years first. Then the war came, and it didn't seem a good time.' When she turned round there was nothing in her face but the familiar derisive amusement. 'You know, only rash creatures like you and Philip would think of starting a family right slap in the middle of Armageddon.'

'Yes, only fools like Phil and me,' said Lucy placidly.

'I've got to get that train,' said Valerie. 'Don't get up.'

'I believe I'll go to Aunt Kitty's after all,' said Lucy suddenly. 'Phil wouldn't want me to take risks.'

When the front door banged, Lucy went to the window and watched her sister walk down the street looking for a taxi. Valerie had got thinner, Lucy noticed; it wasn't difficult to guess the type of lean, rangy Englishwoman she would be in her middle years. Neither had it been difficult to guess, a few minutes back, that she and Bernard had wanted a child ever since their marriage but that no sort of miracle would give them one. Clairvoyance wasn't the prerogative of the kindly women who glanced briefly at Lucy's waistline and then away. Lucy thought that she might go out, too; there was some shopping she wanted to do. When she went to put on her hat, she looked at herself for a moment in the long mirror. She was wearing a print dress with a soft,

gathered bosom, and it struck her that for the first time the lines of her slim figure showed signs of what was happening to her. She surveyed herself from all angles with a sleepy, satisfied smile. As Valerie got thinner, she herself would probably get plumper and prettier, for of course she and Philip would have more babies.

When she boarded a bus at the corner, it was something in her face rather than her figure which made the conductor say, 'Careful now, Ma'am,' and steady her with a hand under the elbow. She moved delicately up the crowded bus and sat down. Newspaper posters strung some tale of horror along the railings, but she looked at them vaguely, thinking that she had better buy some new sweaters for the long, dreaming autumn at Aunt Kitty's.

LUNCH WITH MR. BIDDLE

7 December 1940

Women of all ages liked Winthrop Biddle – 'He's a great dear' was the expression they generally used – and he was devoted to the whole sex in the cosy way of an uncle who enjoys the confidence of a vast number of totally unrelated nieces. His feminine friends knew that he could be relied upon to provide a lunch, a bed, sound advice, or a cast-iron alibi as required, and not to go in for jolly avuncular pouncings in taxis. Never a pouncer even in his youth, in this mellow later phase he was really a perfect example of an elderly English bachelor. Since men liked him, too, his circle of friends and acquaintances was immense. The drawing-room of his small, neat house in Devonshire, where he lived with a devoted housekeeper, was crammed with photographs of charming women and distinguished men inscribed affectionately to their dear old friend Winnie. If they were not actually distinguished themselves, they were sure to be closely related to someone who was; Mr. Biddle had a harmless weakness for people with labels attached.

Before the war he had been an adept at finding unspoilt little places on the Riviera where one could live for a song and where one or another of his women friends – Mme. Delacroix,

who used, you know, to be one of the Derbyshire Melton-Bagburys, or little Mrs. Maverick, whose mother had been, you remember, a famous Edwardian beauty in her day – had a large and hospitable villa. Now that the war had put an end to these excursions, there was nothing for it but to stay at home and sink gracefully, as he himself put it, with his loud, jolly laugh, into a peaceful, gardening old age.

Mr. Biddle's ideas of peace differed considerably, however, from most people's. The spare room at Four Winds was generally occupied by one of a procession of nieces, and Mr. Biddle spent a good deal of time on the telephone inviting his choicer neighbours to little lunch parties or little musical evenings, stiffened, of course, with imported celebrities or near-celebrities from London. 'I do want you to come!' he would shout. 'Effie Trumpington is coming. . . . Of course you know Effie Trumpington. She may not be able to sing for us. You know about her trouble, of course, poor dear.' Satisfied by a polite murmur at the other end of the wire, he would go on to say that he particularly wanted the murmurer's presence at the party because they were going to try out a rather pleasant Alsace wine he had discovered for a song. (Mr. Biddle always arranged some sort of little novelty – a wine or an amusing table decoration or a Provençal way of cooking chicken that his housekeeper really didn't boggle too badly, considering that she had to leave out the truffles and the butter.) 'And I know,' Mr. Biddle would continue, 'what a judge *you* are. Now, I hope you can manage it, my dear fellow. It's such a joy to see people in these dreadful days when one never knows what may happen next. Did you hear the bombs in the night?

I suppose they were after the camp again. I was out half the night – so tiresome! Well, eight o'clock, then. I do trust that I shan't be called out in the middle of dinner by these fearful, inconsiderate bounders.'

The work of an air-raid warden was Mr. Biddle's war effort, and the affectionate adopted nieces thought it really awfully sporting of the dear old thing, clapping a tin hat on his bald head and cycling round the neighbourhood blowing a whistle at all hours. Since Four Winds was surrounded by several juicy military objectives, he was kept pretty busy.

One night an inconsiderate bounder jettisoned a couple of bombs in a field at the bottom of Mr. Biddle's garden, breaking one or two windows of the house and joggling a charming little sketch of St. Tropez off the wall in the dining-room. Mr. Biddle was as ruddy and smiling as ever when describing the incident to his assembled lunch party next day. 'You shall have a peep at the craters after lunch if you're good,' he said to Dora Cunningham, who was there not because she was related to anyone especially distinguished but on the strength of her looks. Mr. Biddle flashed his spectacles and his false teeth at her like an amiable cannibal. 'It makes, I think, rather a nice little contrast,' he said. 'The onslaughts of barbarism in the night, the pleasures of civilisation and beauty today. You're in great good looks, Dora, dear child.' He turned to another guest. 'Tell me what you think of the Amontillado, General. I got it for a song through Bobbie Thrupp – you know, Thrupp & Cantelupe, the wine merchants in St. James's Street. I know, of course, what a judge *you* are.'

The lunch party promised to be wholly successful, Mr. Biddle thought happily. Dora Cunningham, decoratively displaying her legs on the sofa, represented the fair; the brave and the brainy were not forgotten. General Sysonby, looking judicious over the Amontillado, represented the one, and the other was present in the person of Ursula Farmer, a woman novelist who had been bombed out of Hampstead and was now smouldering creatively in a cottage on the common, whence Mr. Biddle had triumphantly unearthed her. The party was completed by Mrs. Sysonby and a Mr. Potts, who was unremarkable in himself but whose aunt had travelled extensively in Tibet. Mr. Biddle, as he went round with the sherry, managed to murmur to General Sysonby, 'You've probably read Ursula Farmer's *Give Us This Day*. Unpleasant stuff but brilliant. No doubt about that.' Leaving the General looking somewhat alarmed, he sketched details rapidly to Miss Farmer. 'Sysonby of the Punjab – magnificent soldier. Grows the best roses of anyone round here.' Dora Cunningham's legs, being self-evident, required no explanation.

Lunch was announced by Mr. Biddle's gardener, who on these occasions was summoned from the herbaceous border and crammed into a black coat. The presence of this heavily breathing servitor gave to the entertainment a native flavour which Mr. Biddle considered every bit as original as the Provençal dishes.

It was not until halfway through the meal that Mr. Biddle realised with dismay that things were not going well. He quickly traced the trouble. Dora, whose business it was to

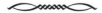

look delectable and keep her mouth shut, had been inspired by the Amontillado or the devil to chip in on Miss Farmer's interesting discussion with General Sysonby about the possibility of invasion. Miss Farmer, who was there to utter, and not to bother about looking delectable, was doing the one all right but was also trying to do the other with an occasional meaningful smile at the General which implied that they must pause for a minute to let the child prattle. The child was beginning to look peevish and unbecomingly flushed.

Mr. Biddle, breathing love and amity, rushed to the rescue by drawing everyone's attention to the centrepiece of flowers, which he had made himself out of bits of shell, cork, and glue. 'It's work that your clever little fingers could do, I know, Dora,' he said, but only Mrs. Sysonby really took an interest. When Mr. Biddle succeeded in disengaging himself from Mrs. Sysonby and was able again to lend an anxious ear to the conversation at the other end of the table, he found that Miss Farmer had led it into deep waters in the hope of shaking off Dora, who, however, had plunged valiantly after her, to the total neglect of Mr. Potts. The General, caught like Paris between Athene and Aphrodite, was twirling his wineglass in glum silence. It seemed possible that the ladies, leaning their panting bosoms nearer, would shortly be growling over him in open conflict on the mat. Really, thought Mr. Biddle despairingly, it was naughty of Dora. No one was performing, and the gardener was being maddeningly slow in handing the *crêpes flambées*, which, Mr. Biddle's nose told him, were burnt.

Happily, Mrs. Sysonby made a diversion by remarking on the Basque table mats, which Mr. Biddle had bought at

Biarritz. 'They make me feel I'm in France,' she said. 'Oh, those winters on the Riviera, Mr. Biddle! When will they ever come again?'

Before Mr. Biddle could answer, Dora had observed that she, for one, didn't care if they never did. 'I wouldn't set foot in that beastly country if you paid me,' she said. 'Of course, you may have some special reason for feeling like that,' said Miss Farmer, smiling at the General and making it sound as though she suspected Dora of having been betrayed by a poilu on a day trip to Boulogne. She went on to say that it was difficult to see how anyone of intelligence – here she paused for a second, which seemed to unhappy Mr. Biddle cruelly interminable – could blame the many for the crimes of the few. Anyone who really knew France and the French, that is. It turned out that Miss Farmer knew France and the French better than they did themselves. Mr. Biddle, miserably chewing cold *crêpes flambées*, had a confused impression that she mentioned a French maternal grandmother, which was awkward, as Dora had just registered her opinion that the French were a low, immoral people whom it was impossible to trust. Clearing his throat, the General began carefully, 'I daresay, when the history fellas come to weigh things up, there will be found to be faults on –' but Dora brushed him aside with a fierce 'I thought that Dunkirk settled it for most people. I had a brother there.'

It seemed that the affair was going to develop into a personal scrap between Dora's brother and Miss Farmer's grandmother. Mr. Biddle noted with alarm that his two embattled guests were rapidly purpling. Something, he felt,

should have warned him – some lack of the essential feminine perfume in Miss Farmer's makeup, some waspishness hidden beneath Dora's delicious exterior – that the mixture was chemically impossible. Casting round desperately for a topic that would offend no one, he remembered Mr. Pott's foot-loose aunt and asked if she had written anything new about Tibet. Mr. Potts was reluctantly transferring his mesmerized attention from the battle of the goddesses to Mr. Biddle when a new voice spoke louder than any at the lunch table.

Never before had Mr. Biddle heard the air-raid siren with sensations of relief and delight. Jumping to his feet, he cried, 'Such a nuisance, but I'll have to go off! Don't disturb yourselves, any of you dear people. Carter is just going to bring coffee.' On his way to the bicycle shed, he put his head in at the dining-room window and called, 'If things get at all noisy, Sysonby, take the ladies under the stairs!'

Bicycling down the drive, settling his tin hat more firmly with one hand, Mr. Biddle had a pleasing vision of Dora and Miss Farmer sitting together under the stairs among his bottles of Amontillado. Since there was nothing like a diversion of this nature for getting people acquainted, the dear ladies would probably emerge cobwebby but the best of friends. The tottering balance of the lunch party had been saved in the nick of time. Really, thought Mr. Biddle happily, he couldn't be more grateful to the siren, which he pictured as yet another niece, even more toothsome than little Dora, sitting on a rock and moaning to oblige old Uncle Winnie. He could hear the inconsiderate bounders zooming faintly

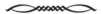

somewhere in the pale-blue sky, and presently the explosion of several bombs. Dora and Miss Farmer would certainly be under the stairs by now, probably holding hands. Spinning along the road, Mr. Biddle put his whistle in his mouth and blew a long, triumphant blast.

BATTLE OF THE GREEKS

8 March 1941

⟨≈≈≈⟩

The Red Cross sewing party met twice a week in Mrs. Ramsay's dining-room to stitch pyjamas, drink a dish of tea, and talk about their menfolk. Mrs. Ramsay found pretty soon that she was in possession of all sorts of unsuspected facts about the husbands of the village – Mrs. Peters' husband, for instance, who was the head groom up at the big house. Mrs. Ramsay felt that she would never be able to look at his neat, gaitered legs and fox-terrier face again without remembering that he had cold feet in bed. 'Ow, terrible!' Mrs. Peters had sighed, rounding off a buttonhole. 'I always say to him, "Daddy," I say, "one might as well put one's feet up against a frog."' It was also interesting to discover that Mr. Lovelace, from Tuppers Farm, had swallowed his auntie's thimble as a child and that Mr. Garner, the big house's second gardener, was always attacked by bees on account of his upstanding hair. Mrs. Ramsay, sitting listening in a white overall so crackling that it hurt, felt she ought to produce some fascinating anecdote about Mr. Ramsay, but could think of none that would bear relating.

There was a day, however, when the conversation took a more international turn. It was impelled that way by Mrs.

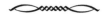

Ramsay's suggestion that the next parcel of comforts might possibly be sent to the Greeks, on whose behalf the wife of the Greek Minister was appealing.

'The Greeks!' said Mrs. Peters suspiciously. 'Ow, what an original idea!' She held up the pair of trousers she was making and regarded them with a frown, as though meditating what it would be like to put one's feet up against a Greek.

The rest of the sewing party looked dubiously at Mrs. Ramsay. The idea of swathing Grecian torsos in good English winceyette was obviously difficult to digest right away. Mrs. Twistle coughed gently. Everything about Mrs. Twistle, who had been in service with a ducal family as a girl, was gentle, even her way of uttering sentiments that would have set the strawberry leaves shuddering with the cold breath of revolution. Mrs. Ramsay could never repress a start when, in a voice soft as a dove's, Mrs. Twistle would murmur, 'There are heads in high places, Madam, as should be rolling on Tower Hill' or 'If I had my way, there are plenty of gentlemen in the present government who I would like – excuse me, Madam – to take out and shoot against a wall.' Having gently coughed, Mrs. Twistle whispered, 'I suppose, Madam, that the Greek gentlemen would be wearing pyjamas? In the photographs they're always in little, short sort of petticoat affairs.'

'Oh dear, Mrs. Twistle! It would be terrible if we sent our lovely pyjamas and then they didn't wear them!' Mrs. Lovelace cried, plucking her glasses off her nose in her agitation.

'Ow, not in bed! They wouldn't wear their petticoats in bed!' Mrs. Peters exclaimed robustly, provoking a choking

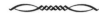

explosion of giggles from Miss Lovelace, the only virgin present in the austere company of matrons.

'Hem this sleeve, Elsie,' said her mother, and the virgin subsided, her face crimson.

Everyone now appealed to Mrs. Ramsay, as the most worldly member of the party, to settle the question of Greek male slumber wear. 'Hark at us all arguing when Mrs. Ramsay can tell us!' cried Mrs. Garner. The table turned its collective gaze upon her, as though confident that she had bedded with half the heroes in *The Iliad*. Mrs. Ramsay thought distractedly of the only Greek in her life, a stout London restaurant proprietor who had stood grilling skewered lamb and garlic over charcoal, wearing neither petticoats nor pyjamas but a stained serge suit. The memory didn't seem really helpful. Happily, she recollected that the Greek Minister's wife had specifically asked for pyjamas, and the party relaxed, breathing heavily.

'Greeks!' said Mrs. Peters. 'Well, wait until I tell Daddy! He'll have a good laugh at me stitching away for the Greeks. Kind of little men, aren't they?' She held up the trousers again. 'I suppose these are going to fit them?'

The garments in question looked to Mrs. Ramsay as though they would accommodate not only a Greek but a couple of Albanians too, but she uttered soothing words.

'Well, poor fellows, it must be bitterly cold up on those mountains,' said Mrs. Lovelace. 'It's sort of nice to think that our pyjamas are going to keep them warm. And when you think how splendid they're being, chasing off that nasty Mussolini –'

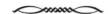

Mrs Twistle coughed gently again and remarked with implacable softness that the Greeks were very marvellous, no doubt, but in her opinion it was a pity that England had to have foreign allies monkeying about with her war.

'Ow well, I'm not all that narrow-minded,' said Mrs. Peters. 'After all, if you have allies, they've got to be foreign. Stands to reason. And as Daddy says, it's not the poor things' fault that they can't speak the King's English proper. We should look nice fools, Mrs. Twistle, parleyvooing in Athens, no doubt. May I trouble you for the box of pins, Mrs. Garner? I thank you.'

Mrs. Twistle's pink cheeks went two shades pinker and her Alexandra coiffure was tremulous with emotion. Her voice, however, remained mild as ever as she whispered that she had nothing against the Greeks, mind you – nothing whatever. 'There's no doubt, Mrs. Peters, that they're a fine lot of men. It's only that if I had my way, we'd have nothing to do with foreigners. We're better off without them, though there are those in high places, I'm well aware, as don't see eye to eye.'

'Ow, and how about the Americans?' Mrs. Peters asked sarcastically. 'I suppose you're going to tell me that if they wanted to come over and help us, you wouldn't let them, on account of them being, as you might say, foreigners.'

'I would not,' replied Mrs. Twistle.

At this interesting juncture, Mrs. Dogberry, who was deaf, shouted out, 'Ready for buttons!' Half a dozen hands reached out cards of buttons to her, and the party settled back again to listen to Mrs. Peters and Mrs. Twistle.

'I'm sure I don't want to contradict you, Mrs. Twistle,' said Mrs. Peters, 'but I must say I think you're wrong. Daddy says that if the Americans came over and fought, we'd have the Nasties beaten before the end of the year.'

'How lovely that would be,' Mrs. Ramsay murmured, hoping to make a diversion.

Mrs. Twistle refused to be side-tracked. 'In my opinion, Mrs. Peters,' she said with ominous calm, 'we should have been better off without the Americans in the last war, if it comes to that.'

'Ow, now, really, Mrs. Twistle!' Mrs. Peters laughed in a superior way. 'Everyone knows that if they hadn't come in when they did, we should have lost the war. And they was a splendid lot of young men. Daddy says –'

'With all due respect to Mr. Peters,' said Mrs. Twistle with chilling stateliness – Mrs. Ramsay, shuddering slightly, could imagine her using the same tone to announce 'Your Grace, the tumbril waits' – 'with *all* due respect, splendid no doubt they was, but uncommon late they was also. By the time they arrived, our boys had done all the work, Mrs. Peters, and there was nothing for them to do. Mr. Twistle always says the same.'

'Ow, there was nothing for them to do, wasn't there?' Mrs. Peters said. 'What about the battles they was in? What about the American war memorial? I suppose they put that up just in memory of the trip across the Atlantic, Mrs. Twistle? Daddy could tell you a very different story. He was right beside the American boys in France, and he says they fought like hellcats, Mrs. Twistle. If you don't mind my saying so,

I think Daddy might be allowed to know better than Mr. Twistle, who wasn't never there. Like hellcats, he said, and you can put that in your pipe and smoke it, Mrs. Twistle. Ow, yes!'

There was now, Mrs. Ramsay observed, not a heave to choose between the Twistle and Peters bosoms. High drama was in the air. Needles were still while the shivering Greeks waited. Miss Lovelace, whose risible faculties seemed equally moved by the Muses of Comedy and Tragedy, gave a sudden wild giggle and was sharply told by her mother to hem a sleeve.

'Pardon me, Mrs. Peters, but my 'usband was there,' Mrs. Twistle said, mislaying, in her agitation, one of the refined 'h's acquired in the ducal household. 'My 'usband was in France from 1915 to 1918.'

'Ow, but behind the lines, Mrs. Twistle, behind the lines,' said Mrs. Peters. 'Daddy was *in* the lines all the time.'

Mrs. Ramsay was waiting apprehensively for Mrs. Twistle's reply to this crushing statement when Mrs. Dogberry suddenly came to the rescue. Having been quietly sewing, blissfully unconscious of the high-voltage currents crackling round her head, she shouted across the table, 'How are chickens laying, Mrs. Twistle? Mine are right off – all the mucky stuff they put in the chicken food nowadays, likely.'

There was a pause, then Mrs. Twistle replied with dignity, 'Thank you, Mrs. Dogberry, but I can't complain. My little pullets are giving me my steady five.'

The crisis was over. Mrs. Ramsay breathed again. Stirring from its drugged trance, the table began to babble of hot mashes and crop-bound hens. A few minutes later, Mrs. Ramsay was electrified to hear Mrs. Peters say magnanimously, 'I passed by your place the other afternoon, Mrs. Twistle, and I thought those Light Sussex birds of yours were looking real lovely.'

'They're nice,' Mrs. Twistle admitted, 'but they don't give the brown eggs like your Rhode Island Reds do, Mrs. Peters.'

When the compliments had died down, Mrs. Ramsay asked cautiously, 'Then it's agreed? We'll send the next lot of pyjamas to the Greeks?'

'Ow, yes, send them to the Greeks by all means,' said Mrs. Peters. 'It'll be a nice change for them to get their limbs into something cosy after those little skirts, poor lads.'

'I think it would be ever so nice, Madam,' said Mrs. Twistle softly. 'After all, they're doing very wonderfully, aren't they? If those in high places don't see that we help them as much as possible, there's heads as will certainly roll when the voice of the people is heard. May I trouble you for the loan of your scissors, Mrs. Peters?'

'Help yourself, Mrs. Twistle,' said Mrs. Peters.

FIN DE SIÈCLE

12 July 1941

It wasn't necessary for Don Merrill to join up; the Ministry of Labour and National Service hadn't called his age group yet. But with the Merrills it was less a question of heroics than of eating or not eating. Because of the war, no one seemed anxious to buy Don's pictures or to let Ernestine design a room. Even if people had the money to spare, they didn't want to spend it on things which, experience had shown, were subject to splintering and mangling. People wanted to buy something solid, a few acres of ground on which to raise chickens and pigs and grow food to eat. 'Safe as houses' was a maxim which meant nothing nowadays with the dust drifting round London, fine brick dust that got in the eyes and made women's black clothes look grey and unfresh. Don went into the Army because he couldn't think what else to do.

Ernestine Merrill had never expected to find herself a soldier's wife. She and Don had both been ardent pacifists right up to Munich, and they had often made disparaging remarks about the military caste. Now here she was, drawing her wife's allowance every week at the post office and liking it. It was wonderful to be able to go out and buy a chop and pay for it instead of getting it on tick because some bitch of a

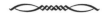

woman hadn't yet paid for having her dining-room done over from Regency to Ernestine Merrill. When she first saw Don in khaki it was a shock, certainly. During peacetime his tastes ran to tough, richly coloured shirts and hairy neckties of peasant inspiration. In his uniform he looked drab as a sparrow, all buttoned up and slicked down.

At first he made little jokes about his new life. It was rather like going back to school, really, he wrote to her. You did what you were told, you ate and slept at regular hours, you began to get keen about all sorts of idiotic things. When he was singled out for a commission, it became apparent that the keenness was real, not ironic. The first few times she heard him talking about 'we' it took her a moment or two to realise that he didn't mean the calm domestic 'we,' Don and Ernestine, but the regiment to which he was going to be attached. Already he had identified himself with it.

He finished his officer-cadet training course and came up to London for seven days' leave before being posted to his unit. On the surface, their life for that week reverted to normal. They got up late, dressed leisurely, and went out every night. The studio, which had acquired a chilly, almost virginal air while Don was away, once more became human with his clothing scattered about, the smell of his pipe and of male food cooking. Ernestine had not realised how bored she was with the scrappy feminine trays she had been languidly fixing for herself.

Picking up the telephone one night, Don said, 'Let's get hold of everyone. I want to talk. God, how I want to talk!'

It was difficult to get a few friends together nowadays – quite ridiculously difficult. The war had a frightening way of making them vanish into thin air. You dialled a number and the phone rang and rang until someone beside you said 'Didn't you know? She's taken the children to New York' or 'Aren't they in Cornwall?' or, rather thoughtfully, 'Of course, it *was* a bad blitz last night.' The Merrills' crowd had been entirely split up. Paul Hathaway, who used to run the precious little Ulysses Press, was a fighter pilot. Elliot Quinn was toting a Home Guard rifle with retired Tory generals in the intervals of his censorship job. Linda was a nurse. Before the war she had been fashion editor of a glossy weekly, going to all the Paris collections, always looking the picture of what more timid women would do their best to look like next season. It was funny seeing her in her unbecoming nurse's cap, her nails short and without varnish. Little Jimmy Shaw, who had shared a house with the Merrills one painting summer near Auxerre, had been killed in action. The list could go on indefinitely. All over London telephone bells were ringing angrily through empty rooms over which the fine brick dust, seeping in at shuttered windows, was beginning to settle.

Most of all, thought Ernestine, the talk for which Don seemed so hungry was different. There was no conversation that wasn't about the war. People talked only of themselves, their jobs, their bombs, their version of Don's new 'we'. She tried to remember what they had talked about before the war. She couldn't. All those good evenings belonged now to the sociologists, the scholars of the future browsing among the remains of the doomed thirties. She wondered if Don

felt the same, but he didn't say anything. In the end they went out to dinner alone. Familiar faces, strange over unfamiliar uniforms, swam into focus through the cigarette haze in the Café Royal. The seven days passed in a flash. She had the feeling that he was really quite pleased to be going back.

After Don left, there seemed to Ernestine to be no point in staying in London, and the next weekend she went down to the country to look for rooms that would be near him. It was a coincidence that Don should be stationed in a place that both he and Ernestine knew well. They had often stayed with Walter and Miriam Brady in the white house that Walter had built on a hill where it could be plainly seen, flashing in the sun, an airy glass insult to the spinsters and the retired colonels of the valley as they looked through their leaded Tudor panes. The house had been a centre for the Merrills' crowd in the old days, but the Bradys weren't there any more. The war had finished Walter's profession as it had finished Don's and Ernestine's. After waiting about for some time in the queue of well-known architects who were hoping for government jobs, he had joined the Air Force and Miriam had taken the boy to Australia. They were two of the friends who had simply vanished.

'Now I know what was wrong with my leave,' Don said. 'Walter wasn't there to talk to. I'd have liked to talk to Walter.'

It was his first admission, Ernestine noticed, that anything at all had been wrong with his leave.

'You won't be bored, because all the other wives are down here too,' he had said when he met her at the train. She

looked at him cautiously. Remarks which six months ago would have been meant ironically were often quite serious now, and she didn't want to laugh when she wasn't supposed to. His face was unsmiling.

'I'm longing to meet them,' she said.

She had brought down a lot of khaki wool and she sat with Don in the little bar of the local pub, knitting a pullover, like all the other women. She hadn't knitted for years and she was slow at it, but it seemed to be the right thing to do. 'Oh, *that* pattern!' the wives would say cosily, dropping into a neighbouring chair. 'I've just done it for Jim. You'll find it a bit of a beast when you come to the neck.' The pub was full of regiment and so was the village, but there were still one or two cottages they might try for rooms, the landlord said as he passed Don's beer and Ernestine's sherry over the counter. 'One of them must be very near the Bradys' place,' Don said.

'Mr. Brady?' said the landlord. 'Ah, he's gone now. In the Air Force, so they tell me.'

'Yes, the last I heard, he was in Egypt,' said Don.

The landlord didn't seem very communicative. Maybe, Ernestine suggested as they finished their drinks and went out, maybe Walter had gone away owing him money. Don said he wouldn't be surprised. It would be more surprising to find someone to whom Walter didn't owe money. They laughed as they thought of him, in his shocking old sweater and sailcloth trousers, going into the pub as though he owned it, shouting for the landlord, and taking away gin and beer for the houseful of thirsty weekend guests.

'Remember that last weekend?' said Ernestine. 'Linda and Jimmy were there. We were all sun-bathing on the terrace and Jimmy was painting Miriam. Remember? It must have been the August just before the war.'

'We might go and look at the house on our way,' Don said. 'I wonder if it's been bought yet. I forgot to ask.'

The first thing they saw as they came round the corner of the familiar lane was a big board, 'For Sale'. Across it a smaller board said despondently, 'No reasonable offer refused'. Don stopped the car.

'Let's take a walk round now,' he said. 'We can go and ask about the rooms afterwards. It's probably those cottages just across the way.'

A man was working in one of the cottage gardens, digging a piece of ground among the apple trees. He stopped working and watched them as they pushed open Walter's gate and walked up the drive. Ernestine was feeling fine because it was a nice day and she was with Don. She looked at him out of the corner of her eye and thought how well and how young he looked in his new uniform. For years he had looked permanently worried. Anxiety had settled in fine lines round his eyes and lips, but now he was tanned and contented, with the contentment of a man who knows where his next meal and a whole settled future of next meals are coming from. Ernestine slipped her hand under his arm, and he looked at her and smiled.

'Poor old Walter,' he said.

She had not been thinking of Walter, and now she looked guiltily at Walter's house. She told herself that all houses

empty for a long time had that same sordid and derelict air. But Walter's house seemed especially forlorn. It looked like something left over from an exhibition, a section of some démodé World's Fair that people would presently come and take down and cart away. They walked round the terrace and peered through the enormous sliding glass walls that Walter had built in defiance of this windy country and the English climate. There was dust on the shining black composition floors; spiders had established a colony in the specially heated vitrines where Miriam had kept her tropical plants.

'It looks funny without the Dufy on that wall,' Ernestine said.

'It looks funniest of all without Walter,' Don said. As if by agreement, they straightened up and walked rapidly down the drive, not looking back.

Yes, Ernestine thought, it's funniest of all without Walter. And without Miriam and Linda and Elliot, Paul and Jimmy and the rest of them. They had gone, and the integrity, the personality of the house had splintered like matchwood. Nobody knew where Walter was. He might be dead. Jimmy was dead, and so were Peter Nash and Nicholas. David had gone to California in the rout of the intellectuals. Lovely Linda was dosing tubercular clerks with cough mixture in a Brixton cellar. Going back to Walter's house had been like visiting a cemetery where there were no tidy tombstones recording beginnings and endings but only question marks over the graves. She looked at Don to see if his flesh was

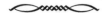

creeping too, and decided that he was thinking of something else. He looked at the view appraisingly as he shut the gate.

'We're having a three-day exercise over this area next week,' he said. 'Tanks and the whole works. It's grand country for tanks.'

'It must be, darling,' she said.

The man digging in the garden opposite had come up to his hedge and was leaning on his spade, waiting for them. 'If you're wanting the key, the agent at Sarumcester has it,' he said.

'We don't want the key,' said Don. 'We were just having a look around.'

The man wiped his face with the back of his hand and nodded cheerfully. He looked Don up and down. 'Ah, it's not the sort of place you'd like, sir,' he said. 'There's many as stops to look, out of curiosity, you might say, but they never wants the key. Who'd be wanting an outlandish place as that is? A regular landmark it is to the bombers, shouldn't wonder, standing out on the hilltop so white and flashing. See it miles off, young fellow in the Air Force tells my son.'

'It could be camouflaged,' Don said.

'Ah, it *could* be,' the man said dubiously. 'But then, think of the blackout, sir! That's what a gentleman who comes to look at it says to me. "Think of all that glass and the blackout," he says. Oh no, it wouldn't do for you and the lady, sir. A funny bunch used to be there – a Mr. Brady and his friends down from London. Yes, a regular funny bunch.' He looked at Don again, friendly and respectful, his blue eyes smiling as they

glanced over the spick-and-span uniform. 'They weren't your sort at all, sir. Not at all.'

Ernestine looked at Don. He was smiling too. She waited for him to explain that they were friends of the Bradys and knew the house well. But instead, he said in a brisk, pleasant voice, 'As a matter of fact, we're not house-hunting at all. We're trying to find a billet for my wife. Perhaps you can tell us where Mrs. Coombes lives?'

LITERARY SCANDAL AT THE SEWING PARTY

6 September 1941

Mrs. Ramsay's Red Cross sewing party did not often stray from the realities of life as they sat in her dining-room stitching pyjamas and assembling the component parts of an elaborate winceyette octopus known as a many-tail bandage. The conversation rarely touched on other topics than the gossip of the little Sussex village, which Mrs. Ramsay had once innocently looked upon as a sleepy hamlet where nothing ever happened. She was now considerably better educated. Sometimes she shivered slightly at the ease with which the ladies kept themselves informed of what was going on beneath every picturesque roof in the place, from the humblest cottage up to the Manor. Mrs. Peters, the wife of the head groom at the big house, seemed to be able to tell when a young wife was 'expecting' even before the young woman had realised it herself, and she had an equally uncomfortable knack of recognising what was sepulchrally termed 'the look' on a doomed person's face. Occasionally Mrs. Ramsay felt that she was sitting in at a sewing bee of the Fates, all busy with shears and thread, snipping at a life here, twining two strands with a knowing cackle there.

Every now and then, however, the conversation reached a more intellectual level. It was on one of these afternoons that Mrs. Twistle dropped her bombshell. She did it gently, for everything about Mrs. Twistle, who had been in ducal service as a girl, was gentle except her opinions, which were frequently of a startling violence. 'When the voice of the people is heard, then, Madam, if you'll excuse me saying so, there's gentlemen in the present government as will find theirselves facing a firing squad' was one of the utterances that Mrs. Ramsay always found a trifle macabre issuing from the lips of a dovelike individual with pink cheeks and an Alexandra fringe.

The afternoon had begun with a little mild chatter about how much better it was to live in one of the old cottages than in the nasty new boxes the Council was putting up when Mrs. Twistle gave the modest cough which generally preceded her entry into the conversation.

'Talking of old houses,' she observed to the company in general, 'reminds me of the old place I was in the first time I ever went out to service, before I was with Her Grace. Oh, it was quaint! Everything was just as it used to be, and the gentleman wouldn't have it modernised on no account. Stella Place was the name of it, over the other side of Foxley Green.'

Mrs. Peters stopped buttonholing. 'Stella Place!' she said with a snort. 'Ow, what a name! Whatever will they think up next? Why not Elsie Place or Maud Place while they're about it?'

'Well, it was on account of its history, Mrs. Peters,' said Mrs. Twistle, smiling indulgently. 'Ever so many years ago

a gentleman called Dean Swift murdered a young lady called Stella there.'

Mrs. Ramsay started violently. So did Mrs. Lovelace, who clutched the pince-nez off her nose and stared with horror at Mrs. Twistle's placid countenance. 'Murdered,' she said faintly. 'How dreadful! If I'd been you, Mrs. Twistle, I shouldn't have been able to sleep a wink in the nasty place.'

'Us girls, being young and silly, used to fancy that we heard something when we came back late from our half-days out,' Mrs. Twistle said. 'Maybe it was the Dean come back, and maybe it wasn't. Anyway, there was the pore lady's blood under the rug on the parlour floor. The parlourmaid let me have a peep one day. They'd tried and tried to get the stains out, she said, but nothing would move them.'

''Uman blood,' Mrs. Garner said. 'Nothing *will* move it. 'Ave you ever been to Stone'enge, Mrs. Twistle? Fred and me went there on a charabang trip one Easter Monday. There's 'uman bloodstains on some of those enormous great stones, so they say, left there by the Druids, and you can't budge them.' To Mrs. Ramsay's slightly dazed fancy, Mrs. Garner appeared to be licking her lips.

'Ow, Druids!' Mrs. Peters exclaimed scornfully, as though she had always suspected them of being a slovenly lot of creatures who wouldn't think of mopping up afterwards. 'All I can say is give me twenty minutes at Stonehenge with a good, stiff brush and some Vim, and I'd get the place so you wouldn't object to eating your dinner off it.'

'No doubt you would, Mrs. Peters,' Mrs. Twistle murmured. 'But the fact remains that I saw the marks with my own eyes, as

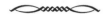

distinct as they was, no doubt, on the day when the pore soul was struck down.'

Needles were suspended while the circle gave its heavily breathing attention to the tragedy. Mrs. Dogberry, who was deaf but had somehow had the facts communicated to her in a series of piercing whispers by her neighbours, suddenly shouted, 'What made Dean bash her, Mrs. Twistle?'

With a meaning glance at Mrs. Lovelace's unmarried daughter, who was sitting with her mouth open, Mrs. Twistle replied, 'Some say one thing and some another, Mrs. Dogberry.'

There was a pause, broken by a wild giggle from Elsie Lovelace, whose risible faculties were frequently out of control. Her mother sighed. 'What a shocking thing!' she said. 'I've heard of Dean Swift, now you mention it. A writer, wasn't he?'

'Ow, writers!' cried Mrs. Peters, as though she lumped the profession with the Druids in one disreputable whole.

'I believe that he wrote the lady letters,' Mrs. Twistle whispered. 'Beautiful letters, hundreds and hundreds of them. I fancy they was printed in a book. It does seem sad that after all that the gentleman should have yielded to such a horrid impulse.'

'Ow, well, perhaps the pore man got tired of waiting for an answer,' Mrs. Peters said, and snickered. 'I remember Daddy used to get wild with me' – the party understood that she was referring to Mr. Peters and not to her paternal ancestor – 'when I was away in service before we were married and he didn't have his weekly letter. I suppose he used to wonder if I wasn't larking with some other boy. Pore Daddy.'

Resisting the impulse to dwell on the vision of Mrs. Peters nubile and larking, Mrs. Ramsay felt that the moment had come to stir from the dreamy trance in which she had been listening and stitching on buttons. 'I *think* you must be confusing Dean Swift with someone else, aren't you, Mrs. Twistle?' she said. 'He certainly wrote letters to someone called Stella, and she certainly died fairly young, but I'm *afraid*' – she smiled apologetically round the table – 'I'm afraid quite naturally.'

The faces of the sewing party expressed a struggle between their desire to believe Mrs. Ramsay, who was held to be a model of elegant culture and book learning, and their faith in Mrs. Twistle, who had seen the nasty evidence under the parlour rug.

Mrs. Peters suddenly made up her mind. 'Ow, of course you're mixing him up, Mrs. Twistle!' she cried. 'Why, he was a dean, wasn't he? Who ever heard of a dean murdering anybody, I'd like to know.'

The others looked thoughtful, as though they were searching their memories for bloody doings at the Deanery. Mrs. Ramsay noted apprehensively that Mrs. Twistle's shining cheeks were a couple of shades rosier as she said, with deceptive softness, 'If you'll forgive me for saying so, Mrs. Peters, I consider as how that is a very unfair idea. Because a gentleman is in high places, there's some people as will never suspect him of doing anything he oughtn't to. If it were Mr. Peters or Mr. Twistle now, it would be a very different story, no doubt.'

'Ow! Daddy murdering someone! That's a good one, I must say,' Mrs. Peters said indignantly.

'Mr. Peters is, after all, only flesh and blood, capable of human passions like the rest,' said Mrs. Twistle.

This was a new and fascinating idea to Mrs. Ramsay, who had hitherto been inclined to think of Mr. Peters as a pair of spindly gaiters and a checked cap. Judging from the expression on Mrs. Peters' face, it was also a new idea to her. She kept a brooding silence for some minutes while the rest of the party sewed furiously and thought of Mr. Peters and human passions.

Mrs. Ramsay was hoping that everything was going to blow over nicely when Mrs. Peters suddenly demanded, 'If the Dean did murder the lady, Mrs. Twistle, I suppose he was took up for it?'

'He was not,' said Mrs. Twistle.

'Ow, now, that settles it that you've got it wrong,' Mrs. Peters said. 'Everybody knows that British justice is going to get you if you do a murder, no matter if you're a dean or Archbishop of Canterbury. Wearing your collar back to front isn't going to make no difference to British justice, Mrs. Twistle. Ow, no, very definitely not!'

'Influence, no doubt, Mrs. Peters,' whispered Mrs. Twistle, calmly enough, but with her Alexandra fringe quivering ominously. 'Influence has been responsible for saving many a gentleman from the common hangman's grave, as you might say. If it had been Mr. Peters, the noose would have been round his neck before the pore lady was cold.'

Mrs. Ramsay intervened hastily. 'Dean Swift is buried in St. Patrick's Cathedral, Dublin,' she said. 'So I'm afraid that shows, doesn't it, that you've got things a little –'

'With a tablet, I daresay,' said Mrs. Twistle bitterly. 'I'm naming no names, but there's plenty of gentlemen lying snug in Westminster Abbey this minute who ought by rights – excuse me, Madam – to be buried at the crossroads with a stake through their black hearts.'

There was a hysterical yelp from Elsie Lovelace and a shocked 'My goodness, what a dreadful idea!' from Mrs. Lovelace, who was fixing a blue striped sleeve into a pink striped armhole in her agitation.

'Bolshie, *I* call it,' said Mrs. Peters, jabbing a needle into her needlecase.

Mrs. Twistle gently patted her fringe. 'As I understand from Mr. Churchill that the Russian gentlemen are now our glorious allies, Mrs. Peters, the term "Bolshie" doesn't quite imply any longer what I take it you *was* trying to imply, Mrs. Peters,' she said.

Mrs. Ramsay was wishing distractedly that the needle-case, with its bristling arsenal winking temptingly, was not still in Mrs. Peters' hand when Mrs. Dogberry sailed into the conversation. Having long since lost any idea of what everyone else was talking about, she introduced one of her abrupt conversational switches by shouting, 'Have you heard that little Mrs. Clark up at Tiggs Farm is expecting again?'

In the ensuing cosy chat, which seemed to Mrs. Ramsay to be a nice blend of robust Elizabethan dialogue and a few extracts from the fertility rites of the aboriginals, the previous topic was happily forgotten. And when the sewing party finally put on their hats and creaked out, Mrs. Ramsay was slightly

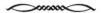

bewildered to see Mrs. Twistle and Mrs. Peters going off up the lane together, apparently on amiable terms and engaged in animated discussion of the best way of keeping colour in gooseberry jam.

GOODBYE, MY LOVE

13 December 1941

Adrian's mother welcomed them as though this were just an ordinary visit, with nothing particular about it. They found her, as they had found her so many times before, working in the big herbaceous border facing the sea, crouching girlishly with a frail little green plant in the palm of one earthy hand. She greeted them abstractedly, pushing back her wispy grey hair with the back of the hand that held the trowel and leaving a smudge. While they talked, Ruth looked at the border, which Adrian had built for his mother on a ledge of the cliff garden, facing it with a paved path beside which the rosemary and the seeded mulleins sprang. Even now, in late autumn, with the sea mist hanging in drops on the spiders' webs that festooned the last red-hot pokers, it was beautiful. Sometimes Ruth wondered if the cold woman, her mother-in-law, didn't express some secret frustration in these savage reds and yellows, these sullen purples, which she caused to gush out of the warm Cornish earth.

Ruth was grateful now for the lack of outward emotion which had so often chilled her. When Mrs. Vyner asked Adrian, as they walked back to the house, 'Which day do you go?' she might have been asking about some weekend visit

he was going to make. He said 'Wednesday', and she repeated 'Wednesday' in a vague voice, her attention wandering to a bough of japonica which the wind had loosened from the wall they were passing. She sat down on the porch to unlace her shocking old gardening boots.

'I suppose you don't know where you're going to be sent,' she said. 'I know it has to be very secret nowadays, because of the submarines.'

'I think it's Syria,' Adrian said. 'From the stuff we're taking, I'm pretty certain.'

'You can't be sure,' Mrs. Vyner said. 'There's a Mrs. Mason who's come to live at the Cross Glens. You know, Adrian, where old Colonel Fox used to live. Well, Captain Mason went off with a topee and shorts, poor man, and the next thing she heard was that he was sitting up on a fiord in Iceland. It's all done to put the spies on the wrong track. I'll point Mrs. Mason out to you in church tomorrow.'

Later, when the Rector came in, he made more of an occasion of it than his wife had. He gave Ruth a heartier kiss than usual. 'It's good of you to think of the old people when you've got so little time left,' he said. Ruth disliked the phrase 'so little time left'. Suddenly she was inordinately conscious of time. The house was full of it, ticking between simpering shepherdesses on the mantelpiece, grumbling out of the tall mahogany case in the hall, nervously stuttering against Adrian's wrist. The church clock, just across the rectory garden, struck every quarter. Ruth thought, 'Four days, and one of them nearly gone.'

After dinner the Rector got out *The Times* atlas and pored

over it with Adrian, while Mrs. Vyner sat knitting a sock and talking about the garden and the village. The Rector's broad thumb, tracing the possible course that a convoy would take out into the Atlantic, swooped down upon the Cape. He and Adrian sounded quiet and contented, as though they were plotting a fishing holiday.

Ruth and her mother-in-law sat knitting a little apart, chatting in low voices.

'The black spot has been dreadful on the roses this year,' Mrs. Vyner said. 'Really dreadful. What do you plan to do after he's gone?'

'I shall get a job,' Ruth said. 'I thought I might go into one of the services. Shorthand and typing ought to be useful. Anyway, I'm going to do something.'

'That's sensible,' Mrs. Vyner said. 'After all, you'll be perfectly free, won't you? It isn't as though you have any ties.'

'No, I've got no ties at all,' Ruth said.

When they were undressing in the big, chilly guest room, she said to Adrian, 'Somehow, now that you're going I wish we'd had a child. You know, the Sonnets and all that – "And nothing 'gainst Time's scythe can make defence, Save breed, to brave him when he takes thee hence."'

'I'm not sorry,' Adrian said. 'This way I shan't be missing anything. When I get back we'll have the fun of kids together.'

'Yes, we will,' Ruth said, raising her voice slightly, as though she were talking to someone behind him. 'How long do you think the war's going to last?' she asked, picking up her hairbrush.

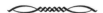

'Darling! As though it matters a damn what I think. I don't know – maybe another couple of years or so.'

'Some people say it will be over next spring.'

'Some people talk a hell of a lot of nonsense,' he said.

The bed was a big, old-fashioned double, its mattress divided into two gentle troughs where successive generations of guests had lain. Ruth got in and pulled the covers up to her chin. She watched Adrian moving around the room. 'They were an awful long time demobilising people after the last war, weren't they?' she said. 'Maybe the firm would make a special application for you, or whatever they do. After all, they'll be terribly anxious to get you back. Mr. Hobday told me himself that he didn't know how they were going to get on without you.'

'Oh, they'll manage,' Adrian said.

At intervals all through the night, Ruth kept waking up and listening to the sea. She pictured it running up the jagged inlets of the long, cruel coast, along which she and Adrian had often sailed in his little boat. He was asleep, breathing softly and lightly, his face close to her shoulder. She lay thinking this way until it began to get light and the birds started shouting in Mrs. Vyner's wild garden.

They went to church next morning, walking through the gate in the yew hedge into the bleak little churchyard. The congregation that had come to hear the Rector preach was small and badly dressed, for the parish was thinly populated and poor. It was easy, without Mrs. Vyner's whisper, to identify the more prosperous Mrs. Mason, tweedy in a front pew, with a plain little girl on either side. Captain Mason had at least provided her with two defences 'gainst Time's scythe, hideous though they were in their spectacles and with gold bands round their teeth, before he took himself off to his Icelandic fiords. Ruth looked across the aisle at Mrs. Mason, who was cheerfully singing the Te Deum. 'I'll get used to it, too,' she thought. The only other representative of the local gentry in church was Major Collingwood, who read the lessons in a voice beautifully husky with Irish whisky and buttonholed Adrian afterwards in the porch. 'Well, my boy! Just off, I hear,' he said. 'Going East, I suppose? No, no, don't tell me – mustn't ask, mustn't ask. Well, it looks like a big showdown there this winter. Hitler's going to try and break through. Yes, we've got to be prepared for heavy fighting, heavy fighting.'

'The old fool,' Ruth thought. She walked away and began reading some of the inscriptions on the crosses of local grey stone at the heads of the few green mounds in the churchyard. Most of the men were fishermen who had been drowned in winter storms along the coast. 'John Tregarthen, who lost his life off Black Point, 10 December 1897,' she read. 'Samuel Cotter, drowned in the wreck of the Lady May, 25 January 1902.'

Adrian came up and took her arm. 'Hungry?' he asked. She shook her head, and he saw that there were tears in her eyes. 'Damn that old idiot!' he said. 'Darling, it's going to be a quiet winter. What do you bet? We'll be stuck in some bloody desert, eating our heads off with boredom. We're going to be forgotten men, forgotten by Hitler, forgotten by the General Staff, forgotten by –'

'It's all right,' she said.

Mrs. Vyner came up, fastening her shabby fur round her long, thin neck, and the three of them walked back into the rectory garden.

Next day, Ruth and Adrian went back to London. That night they went out with friends and had plenty to drink. Ruth was able to sleep that night. The next evening, their last, they dined quietly in the flat. She had cooked the things he liked best, but neither of them had much appetite. At last they gave up trying. The one clock in the flat went on sucking time, like an endless string of macaroni, into its bright, vacant face. Every clock in London seemed to crash out the quarters outside their drawn curtains. When the telephone rang as they sat over their coffee, Adrian got up to answer it as though he were glad of the interruption. It turned out to be a man who used to be in love with Ruth and who had been out of England for some time. Adrian had always disliked him, but he sounded very cordial now. Afterwards he said, 'I'm glad Mike has turned up again. I want you to go out with him. That's why I said to him just now, "When I'm gone I'd take it as a personal favour if you'd give Ruth a ring now and then and take her out and give her a good time."'

'I don't want to go out with Mike,' she said.

'Please do,' he said. 'It will make me feel better to think of you looking pretty, out dancing and enjoying yourself.'

The following morning there was plenty to do – breakfast, a taxi, last-minute things. Meeting at some moment in the bustling, efficient nightmare, Adrian said, 'I don't suppose I'll be able to wire you, but I'll give someone a letter to post from the port after we sail,' and Ruth said, 'That will be fine.' She felt cold and frightened and a little sick, as though this were the morning fixed for a major operation. She wasn't going to the station, so they said goodbye in the hall, a tiny cupboard built for a man to hang his hat in, for a woman to read a telephone message in – not for heroic partings.

'Well, take care of yourself,' Adrian said. 'Don't forget what we said last night. If the bombings start again, you go down to Cornwall, you go anywhere. Anyway, you get out of here. Promise? Otherwise I won't be able to keep my mind on this war.'

'I promise,' Ruth said, smiling. Language was inadequate, after all. One used the same words for a parting which might be for years, which might end in death, as one did for an overnight business trip. She put her arms tightly round him and said, 'Good-bye, my love.'

'Darling,' he said. 'I can't begin to tell you –'

'Don't,' she said. 'Don't.'

The door shut, and presently Ruth heard the taxi driving away. She went back into the living-room, sat down, and looked at the breakfast things. Adrian's cup was still half full of coffee, a cigarette stubbed out in the wet saucer. The cigarette seemed to have acquired a significance, to be the kind of relic which in another age would have been put carefully away in a little box with the toenail parings of a dead man, the hair clippings of a dead woman.

The next two days were bad. Ruth felt that the major operation had come off but that she still had not come round from the anaesthetic. She pottered about the flat, went for

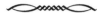

a walk, bought some things she wanted, dropped in at a film and a concert. Time now seemed to have receded, to be an enormous empty room which she must furnish, like any other aimless woman, with celluloid shadows of other people's happiness, with music that worked one up for nothing. An hour or so after Adrian left, she put through a call to Cornwall. 'Adrian's gone,' she said, and across the bad line, across a rival conversation between two men who were trying to arrange a board meeting, she heard her mother-in-law's calm, tired voice saying, 'Yes, it's Wednesday, isn't it? I knew he was going on Wednesday.' As she hung up the receiver, she suddenly remembered a French governess out of her childhood who used to rage, weeping with anger, 'Oh, you British, you British!' Her friends rang her up with careful, planned kindness. Their stock opening was 'Has he gone? Oh, you poor darling! But aren't you terribly relieved it's over?' and then they would ask her to a dinner or a theatre. Their manner was caressing but sprightly, as though she were a stretcher case who mustn't be allowed to know that she was suffering from shock. She slept very badly and had terrible dreams, into which the sea always seemed to come. She went to sleep picturing the blacked-out ship creeping out cautiously into the dark sea. The girl who washed her hair had once told her that her brother had been torpedoed off Norway and that he had been rescued, covered with oil from the explosion. In one of Ruth's dreams Adrian was struggling in a sea of oil while Mrs. Vyner, watching from her cliff garden, said 'Yes, it's Wednesday, isn't it? I knew he was going to drown on Wednesday.'

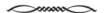

On the third day, Ruth woke up feeling different. It was a queer feeling, exhausted but peaceful, as though her temperature had fallen for the first time after days of high fever. The end of something had been reached, the limit of some capacity for suffering. Nothing would be quite as bad again. She thought, 'After all, there are thousands of women going through what I'm going through and they don't make a fuss.' She got up and dressed, with particular care, because she planned to go round to one of the women's recruiting stations today and find out about a job. It would be important to make a good impression at the first interview. Afterwards she would write a funny letter about it to Adrian, she thought. Although it would probably be months before any mail caught up with him, she would write tonight and tell him not to worry, that she had finished making a fuss and was being sensible, like all the other women in England – like Mrs. Mason, the jolly woman in tweeds singing away at the Te Deum as though there were still something to be thankful about.

She was out all day, and when she put her latchkey in the door she was humming. As she took off her hat, the telephone rang, and she went to it, still humming, and said 'Hello?' Adrian's voice said 'Darling?' and her knees went weak. She sat down suddenly, while his voice raced on, sounding excited and a bit blurred, as though he had had two or three drinks. 'I'm at the station, I'll be right round. Got to the port, but something went wrong. We all waited, then the message came through that it was cancelled. I wasn't allowed to phone you.'

'Cancelled?' she said stupidly. 'You're not going?'

'Not for another week,' he said. 'Maybe ten days. God, what luck. I'm going out to find a taxi. Darling, don't move until I get there.'

Ruth heard the click as he hung up, and she hung up slowly, too. For a moment she sat quite still. The clock on the table beside her sounded deafening again, beginning to mark off the ten days at the end of which terror was the red light at the end of the tunnel. Then her face became drawn and, putting her hands over it, she burst into tears.

WAR AMONG STRANGERS

17 January 1942

~~~~~~~~~~~~

On the day that war broke out between the United States and Japan, Mrs. Bristowe rang up her husband at his Ministry in London. She was at home in Hampshire, and the call took some time to come through. The line was busy, probably with other agitated telephonings, thought Mrs. Bristowe, trying not to pace up and down the room like a caged animal. If only John were here to be soothing and sensible. The night before she had sat by the radio alone, listening to the details of the Japanese attack, taking them in with part of her mind while her thoughts flew in dismay to her two children, Simon and Janet, small and stranded and precious, in California.

Ordinarily the phone was never quiet; now it was mute, its mum blackness suddenly as hostile as an unfriendly face. She began to prowl again, listening abstractedly to Mrs. Prout banging a brush against the staircase banisters out in the hall. Mounted on a terrifying old bicycle, Mrs. Prout sailed up from the village every day to oblige Mrs. Bristowe. With the children not there and John in London all the week, it was easy enough to jog along that way.

The phone rang suddenly, and Mrs. Bristowe's lunge towards it sent a scatter of books and knitting off the table. As she picked up the receiver, the voice of the Ministry switch-board girl chirped in her ear, and after a pause John's voice said 'Hello'.

'Oh, darling,' she said, 'I was afraid you might be at a conference or something.'

'No, I'm not at a conference. What's the trouble, Barbara?'

Mrs. Bristowe found herself fighting back tears as she said, 'This awful news!'

'What? I don't hear you very well.'

'I said this awful news,' Mrs. Bristowe repeated, raising her voice.

'Oh, well, it wasn't entirely unexpected, was it?'

'John, I'm so dreadfully worried about the children. I didn't sleep a wink last night.'

'I don't think you need worry,' he said. 'I really don't. From what we know of them, the Maddisons seem thoroughly good, solid people. I'm sure they'll look after the kids all right, whatever happens.'

'But it mayn't be safe for them to stay with the Maddisons,' Mrs. Bristowe said. 'They may evacuate all the children from that area if things look bad. If only there was some way of getting at them!'

'Well, there isn't, I'm afraid. We can cable Mrs. Maddison, of course, and ask for news. Cables are going through without much delay,' he added in his Ministry voice.

Mrs. Bristowe had the peevish sensation that she was listening to a Civil Service pamphlet, one of the bracing kind that was pushed in at the door with the mail and told you to stay put, to keep off the roads during invasion, and to avoid

panic and despondency. What she had wanted, ever since that awful moment last evening, was a bosom on which to lean and cry, not a bit of brisk, official buff paper. She said crossly, 'I suppose Germany's going to declare war on them next.'

'It certainly looks like it.'

'I ought never to have allowed the children to go without Nanny. Never, never! Or I ought to have gone with them myself.'

'Now, darling! You know you didn't want to leave your job in the W.V.S.'

'Oh, damn the W.V.S.!' she cried, and hung up.

A moment later she regretted it, but by then it was impossible to do anything. Another call, to tell John she was sorry, to receive his amused forgiveness, would make her hopelessly late for the canteen.

She ran upstairs to get her hat and was halted in the bedroom, as though by a blow over the heart, by the photograph of the children on her dressing table. It was the latest snapshot, taken by Mrs. Maddison on Simon's birthday and sent over with a long, careful letter describing his presents, the children who had come to tea, what he had said, what Janet had worn. Certainly, Mrs. Maddison did the thing handsomely – regular cables, details of gains in height and weight, school reports, copious snapshots. Now that her children weren't here, Mrs. Bristowe seemed to know far more about them than she ever had before.

She sat down, the photograph in her hand, the canteen forgotten. The children looked very fair and English in the clear American sunlight, Simon in his shorts and jersey, Janet

in her smock from Liberty's. The tears came into Mrs. Bristowe's eyes again, and refused to be pushed back, as she thought of the last time she had seen her children, that dreadful morning at the port from which they had sailed. They had seemed terribly small then as she stood beside them, making inane remarks to their escort, a jolly Girton girl who looked, thank God, as though she would be good at swimming. The time which elapsed before Mrs. Bristowe got the cable saying that they had arrived safely was the worst torture she had ever known. Torture was really a novelty to her, the placidly contented wife of a permanent Civil Servant, but she had made up for all arrears of suffering in a single bound. Was she going to have to go through all that over again? John had seemed maddeningly smug about the Maddisons, but how could you be certain how people were going to behave in an emergency? Letters and photographs didn't tell you anything, really. No, thought Mrs. Bristowe wretchedly, she had sent her children into a war among strangers. Kind strangers, but strangers all the same.

The striking of a clock reminded Mrs. Bristowe that they would soon be ringing up from the canteen to find out what had happened to her. She ran downstairs and called to Mrs. Prout, 'Back for tea. If a cable comes over the telephone, take it down carefully.' Then she sprinted for the bicycle shed.

Next to her at the canteen that morning, scraping carrots and scrubbing potatoes, was a chatty Mrs. Warner, who immediately cried, 'Oh, my dear, I've thought so much about you! Aren't you worried sick about your Simon and Janet,

right out there in the middle of it all?' And another helper said, 'I was only saying to Dick last night, "Thank goodness we didn't send Brian and Peter over that time." Somehow, I always felt one ought to keep them here, even when things looked so bad.' She sounded pleased with herself, as though conscious of having behaved like a Roman matron while Mrs. Bristowe had ratted on the British Empire. The professional cook, who spoke in a refined voice with pinched vowels to show that she was really a lady and no mistake, sighed, 'Oh, dear, Ay must say Ay see no end to it now, do you? Ay feel that it will be years and years. Ay do really, Mrs. Bristowe.' When the school children arrived for lunch, it wasn't much better. All these shaggy heads, these sturdy little bodies tucking into the soup and dumplings, made Mrs. Bristowe feel terrible. Most of the children were evacuees from Portsmouth, but their mothers could get into a train and come up and see them whenever they wanted. There wasn't an enormous stretch of water, a continent, and a new war between them.

When Mrs. Bristowe got home and wearily opened the front door, the first thing that she heard was a crash of breaking china. For some reason, this sound of domestic disaster was the culmination of the day, the final touch to the tale of despair. She went along to the kitchen and found Mrs. Prout on hands and knees, sweeping up the fragments of the afternoon-tea tray. 'Really!' Mrs. Bristowe said, her voice shaking with unaccustomed anger. 'I must say I do think this is careless! I'll never be able to match it – never. I suppose you don't realise how impossible it is to get this sort of thing now? Mr. Bristowe has always been particularly fond of that tea service.' She did not wait to hear anything that Mrs. Prout might have to say but turned and stalked out of the kitchen, back to the quiet, neat sitting room, where there was no longer danger of taking a header over the children's litter, back to the telephone which wouldn't ring, the radio which would focus her lonely evening to a pinpoint of terror.

After a while she heard Mrs. Prout coming heavily along the passage, bringing a newly assembled tea tray and wheezing with anxiety as she negotiated the doorpost. Mrs. Prout set the tray down beside Mrs. Bristowe and straightened up, sighing and smoothing her apron. She was a stout woman with steel-rimmed glasses set across a small red button of a nose, which peeped out between glossy red knobs of cheeks.

'I'm ever so sorry about the tea set, Madam,' she said. 'I don't know how I could have been so clumsy, I'm sure. It must be because my mind's not on things on account of thinking about Rose.'

'Rose?' said Mrs. Bristowe.

'Our girl, Rose. The one that went for a nurse to Singapore. The news has given me a turn, as you might say. I don't trust them yellow monkeys, them Japanese. They won't fight clean, I said to Prout.'

'Look,' said Mrs. Bristowe. 'Go and get another cup and sit down and have a cup of tea with me. It'll do us good.' Mrs. Prout looked startled, and Mrs. Bristowe had to snap at her 'Oh, go on, do!' before she creaked reluctantly out of the room. Those who talk of English class distinctions, thought

Mrs. Bristowe in some exasperation, ought to get it quite clear who draws the distinctions.

When Mrs. Prout returned with the cup and saucer, she coughed and murmured 'Excuse me' and seated herself on the edge of an armchair. Pouring out the tea, Mrs. Bristowe said, 'I'm sorry I was cross just now. The truth is I'm worried to death about my children, too. It's horrid feeling that they're in the war again, and without me this time.'

'Tchk!' Mrs. Prout clicked her tongue sympathetically against her fine, porcelain teeth. 'Well, Prout says it's no good worrying. We can't do anything, he says.'

'So does Mr. Bristowe.'

'I didn't feel easy in my mind when Rose went, but she was all set on it. She looked nice in her uniform, I will say. White. Ever such a bother to keep clean, you'd think, but I suppose there's not many smuts out there.'

'What I hope is that they don't come in for any air raids,' Mrs. Bristowe said. 'Somehow, the thought of air raids there seems worse than air raids here – I don't know why. Probably because we're used to them. And Simon would mind. Janet is solid as a rock, but Simon would be frightened.'

'Ar, poor little dear! Well, our Rose has never been frightened of anything. If she gets hold of any of them Japs, she'll tell them off all right. I can just hear her!' Mrs. Prout chuckled richly, plastering one knuckly red hand across her mouth.

It began to get dark. They sat on, speaking their thoughts aloud, courteously waiting for each other to finish, returning to their separate thought tracks. A dim comfort had begun to flow from Mrs. Prout to Mrs. Bristowe, the same sort of comfort she remembered in her childhood. Then a thin night-time wail for help had brought an instant, subterranean upheaval from the other bed, the splutter of a match, the apparition of her nurse in a red flannel dressing-gown, with steel-rimmed glasses on a kind, red face like Mrs. Prout's. Then all of life had been – as one could fool oneself into thinking this moment was – safe firelight, the ticking of a clock telling time that would last forever, the radio not invented, Japan a squiggle on the map, suffering something that happened to grown-ups in books.

Mrs. Prout stirred and sighed. 'Well, one of these days we'll all have a good laugh thinking of these times. You'll have your little pair back, Mrs. Bristowe, and we'll have our Rose, and Hitler and that nasty snake of an emperor will have the ropes round their necks, as they richly deserve. Until then, as Prout says, there's nothing to do but get on with it.' She struggled to her feet. 'My word, I'll have to do the blackout and pop home, or else Prout will be thinking I've met one of them soldiers in a dark lane.'

Presently she put her head round the door. 'Just off,' she said. 'Sure you're all right, Madam?' she added, to show that the intimacy of the last hour was at an end.

'Quite all right,' Mrs. Bristowe said.

Mrs. Prout had not been gone long when the phone rang. It was John.

'That you, Barbara? It struck me that I wasn't as

sympathetic as I might have been this morning, darling. Ancaster was in the room and it happened to be – anyway, I'm sorry I was terse.'

'I'm sorry I hung up on you.'

'I thought you'd like to know that I've sent a long cable to the Maddisons. We ought to hear pretty soon, I should think.' He gave an awkward cough. 'Until then, my dear, chin up and keep smiling, won't you?'

Mrs. Bristowe felt that she was being dished out another pamphlet, but she said, 'I'll try. All we can do is get on with it, I suppose.'

'Exactly,' he said in a relieved voice. 'Just what I said this morning. Well, darling, I'll try to get down midweek if the old boy isn't tiresome. Ring me if the Maddisons' answer comes before then, won't you?

When she had hung up the receiver the clock was striking six. She went over to the radio, turned the knob, and sat down with all the other anxious women to knit and listen.

COMBINED OPERATIONS

29 August 1942

〜⚬〜

Gregory Parsons opened the gate of his Oxfordshire cottage and trod delicately up the path between the clipped lavender hedges. It was a beautiful summer evening and he looked warm and a trifle dusty in his dark town clothes. He had taken off his black Homburg hat as he walked from the station, and carried it in his hand, together with the evening paper and a large government briefcase. At the door he paused, then cautiously lifted the latch and entered his home as though proposing to make off with the silver.

His wife, Laura, wearing a red-and-white striped blouse and dark-blue slacks, came into the dark little flagstoned hall, carrying a bowl of raspberries. 'You needn't worry,' she said. 'They're down at the pub.'

'Thank God for that!' said Gregory. He dropped his hat, newspaper, and briefcase in a heap on the floor and took off his coat, making a not very successful shot with it in the direction of a chair. Then he followed her into the kitchen, where she was filling a row of bottling jars with the raspberries.

'Well?' he said. 'How did they take it?'

'Perfectly all right,' she said. 'They didn't even seem surprised.'

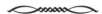

'When are they –'

'The day after tomorrow. Roger says he's due for a week's leave anyway, and they think they'll go off to Wales and fish. Then they're going to try and get the Murdochs to lend them their studio for a bit.'

'Trust Roger to try and get something on the cheap. Thursday! My God, I can hardly believe it.' Gregory stretched out his arms luxuriously, and a look of utter peace came over his nervous, sallow face. 'I couldn't keep my mind on anything today. There was a conference this afternoon, rather an important one. All through it I kept on thinking, what the hell shall we do if they dig their toes in and say they won't go?'

'It was easy, really,' Laura said, snapping rubber rings carefully round the bottles. 'I broke it to Madeline this morning when at last she condescended to get herself out of bed and come downstairs. She was scratching round here making herself some coffee when I did it. I said, "Oh, Mad, Gregory and I feel like beasts, but we've got to ask you and Roger to turn out. Gregory's sister Penelope and her children are coming over from Ireland, and they haven't got another place to go except us."'

'It sounds a bit fishy,' said Gregory. 'They know Penelope and I can't stand the sight of each other. However, I expect you put it over all right. What did she say?'

'She said, "Of course, my dear. That was in the arrangement when we came here. You promised to let us know when anything like that turned up." All very reasonable, I must say. It made me feel rather dreadful. Then, when Roger got back this evening, she sidetracked him upstairs and told him. I

heard their voices for ages when I was picking the raspberries. Then they came down, and Roger said about Wales and the Murdochs' studio, and they went off to the pub.'

'Leaving you picking the raspberries,' said Gregory bitterly. '*Of* course. If that bitch had ever done a hand's turn around here to help you, things might have been very different.'

'Oh, I'd really rather do it,' said Laura. 'You know the *fuss*. Besides, they're not going to eat these raspberries, are they?'

'No, by God, they're not,' said Gregory cheerfully. 'Now that they're going –' He stopped and repeated the words, as though he were rolling them on the tongue like some rare old vintage. 'Now that they're going, it's amusing to try and decide what got us down worst. Do you know, with me I think it's Roger's habit of handing me the vegetables at meals. Handing them to me as though I were a guest in my own house, mark you.'

'The way Mad leaves the bathroom!' said Laura. 'It certainly will be nice to go in and not find clouds of powder over the glass, everything swimming in water, and the lavatory jammed with face tissues.'

'It will also be pleasant to turn the radio to the programme *we* want for a change,' said Gregory.

He got up and went out into the hall. Picking up his briefcase, he waved it at Laura and said, 'I've got two bars of chocolate in here – that little shop off the Strand had some in today.'

'Darling, how lovely! We'll eat it when we go to bed.'

'Soon we'll be able to eat it when and where we like,' said Gregory. 'Well, I'm going to change. You know, it's indescribable how different the house feels when they're out of it.' Trolling *Figaro* unmusically but happily, he climbed the rickety stairs to their bedroom. There he got out of his London clothes, letting them lie where they dropped, and put on a loud coloured shirt and a pair of dirty grey flannel trousers. Then he went downstairs and out into the garden, where he fetched a hoe from the lean-to shed and ambled off to the vegetable plot.

Gregory began hoeing the bind-weed among the carrot rows, enjoying the small, muscular effort after the long day of sitting at his desk and in the hot, crowded train. The carrots were looking fine. 'Next year,' Roger had said the other day, 'we must find room for more carrots and cut out the turnips. Neither Mad nor I like turnips.' Like his damned nerve, thought Gregory, without bitterness. The time for bitterness was over and past. This was the weak and delicious period of convalescence, when it was pleasant to lie back and think dreamily how much had been endured. Now that the temperature was down, it was possible for the first time to analyse coolly, and that in itself was a luxury. Since the Butlers had moved into Willow Cottage, Gregory couldn't remember feeling cool and analytical once. Yet it had seemed such an admirable arrangement at the start. He and Laura had always got on splendidly with Roger and Madeline. They had dined with each other regularly, and Roger and Gregory worked in the same Ministry. Gregory had even felt faintly and

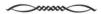

agreeably attracted by Madeline, who was blonde and pretty as a bad picture, without the bother of ever having to do anything about it. When the Butlers' flat was blitzed, therefore, it seemed a fine idea that they should move out into the country with the Parsons. Gregory couldn't put his finger right on the moment when it had stopped being a fine idea and become hell. Neither could he point triumphantly to any big contributing cause. If anyone had asked him, he would have had to say, 'Well, it's partly the way Roger begins every other sentence with "In point of fact", and Mad talks brightly at breakfast, and Roger is always in the lavatory when I go there, and he gets our bottles of gin mixed, and Mad rings up friends of hers in Cheshire or somewhere and forgets to pay for the calls.' Half the time it wasn't even as definite as that. It was a laugh, a way Mad had of sitting, a glance exchanged between her and Roger, which was sufficient to set Gregory's teeth on edge. Maybe he had exaggerated some of it now and then. For instance, in this mood of splendid, almost lightheaded detachment which had come over him as he hoed the carrot rows, he knew that quite possibly Madeline hadn't eaten his butter ration a few days before. Yet he could remember how, at the time, the pat had definitely looked smaller to him than when he had seen it last, and how he had confided to Laura in bed that night that he was positive that Madeline had helped herself from it for the sandwich she had suddenly felt like making the night before. He had shaken with anger, thinking of his butter disappearing into that wide, peasant mouth, which had once seemed to him aimlessly desirable. Rather idiotic, sordid little emotions they seemed now. He and Laura had never been able to talk freely except in bed. Willow Cottage wasn't like a large house, where you could get away easily from other people. It was old, too, and sounds bounced through the leaks in its beams and wattle-and-daub walls. As they lay with the covers drawn up to their chins and talked in furious low voices, they could hear the Butlers murmuring away in the next room like furtive doves under their eaves.

Roger and Madeline walked up the path between the lavender to Willow Cottage. They were arm in arm and feeling very affectionate and happy, for they had been celebrating down at the Bull. Suddenly it had seemed an occasion for celebration, and they had stayed on and on in the stuffy little bar, with its darts board and picture of Queen Victoria as a girl. 'In point of fact,' Roger had said as he brought over their third pint, 'poor Laura's nothing but an Andromeda of the sink, with no Perseus in sight. A certain amount of household toil is inevitable in these days, but is it necessary to make quite such a tiresomely conspicuous sacrifice of oneself?' They had decided that it wasn't and that Thursday would be a merciful deliverance all round. When they went into the cottage the first thing they saw was Gregory's hat, newspaper, and coat lying on the floor. Roger nodded at them. 'Typical Gregory,' he said in a low voice. 'Just as we were saying. Charming when you don't have to live with it, no doubt.' He picked up the hat and put it carefully on the table just as Laura came out of the kitchen and said, 'There you are, you two.'

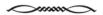

'Yes, here we are,' said Madeline. She and Roger exchanged a slight smile. Sitting at Queen Victoria's feet, they had found out that Laura's habit of stating the obvious was one of the things that made them both want to scream.

Supper was an amiable meal, at which the approaching departure was mentioned lightly by both couples. Roger said that being in London again would have its advantages. 'In point of fact, the train journey is a bit of a sweat,' he said, getting up and handing Gregory the dish of peas. 'Thanks, Roger,' said Gregory mildly, helping himself. After supper they went into the living-room, and Roger fiddled with the radio until he found a programme of swing. Ordinarily Gregory detested swing music, but tonight he wagged his foot and hummed.

'I suppose you'll want old Carter and his taxi to take your stuff to the station on Thursday,' he said.

'I suppose so,' said Roger.

Gregory hummed some more. He and Laura went to bed early. They sat up in bed, reading and eating the two bars of chocolate with private, deliberate greed. They could hear the Butlers in the next room, talking in low voices, Roger cleaning his teeth and gargling, and the scratchy sound of Madeline brushing out her thick, fair hair.

Any one of these noises would have been calculated, twenty-four hours before, to make Gregory irritable, but now he listened dreamily. It was nice to think of Madeline brushing her light hair in the candlelight. The silly creature had nearly set the thatch on fire one night a few weeks back,

but he thought of that incident only momentarily. He was thinking of her sunburnt arms raised as she brushed, pulling taut the lines of that really delectable bosom. 'I hope it will come off all right Thursday,' he said.

'It will come off all right,' said Laura comfortably. 'Don't you worry.' She shut up her book and snuggled down beside him.

Gregory blew out the candle and lay down, too. He felt very happy. Already he could look ahead with anticipation to the time when he would again feel that particular need which the Butlers had always filled so satisfyingly, when he would pick up the telephone and say 'Roger? Look, what are you and Mad doing tonight?'

GOOD EVENING, MRS. CRAVEN

5 December 1942

⌒⟡⌒

For years now they had been going to Porter's, in one of the little side streets off the Strand. They had their own particular table in the far corner of the upstairs room, cosily near the fire in winter, cooled in summer by a window at their backs, through which drifted soot and the remote bumble of traffic. Everything contemporary seemed remote at Porter's. The whole place looked as though it had been soaked in Madeira – the rich brown walls crowded with signed photographs of Irving and Bancroft and Forbes-Robertson, the plush seats, the fly-spotted marble Muses forever turning their classic noses hopefully towards the door, as though expecting to see Ellen Terry come in. The waiters were all very old. They carried enormous napkins over their arms and produced the menu with a special flourish from the tails of their old-fashioned coats. The waiter who attended to the corner table looked as though he could have walked on as a senator in a Lyceum production of *Julius Caesar*. Leaning protectively over them, he would say in a hoarse, fruity voice, into which Madeira seemed to have seeped too, 'The steak-and-kidney pudding is just as you like it today, Mr. Craven.'

Every Thursday evening, wet or fine, they would be dining in their corner under the bust of Mrs. Siddons, talking quietly, sometimes holding hands under the tablecloth. It was the evening when he was supposed to have a standing engagement to play bridge at his club. Sometimes he called for her at her flat; more often they arrived separately. Out of all their Thursdays she loved the foggy winter evenings best, when the taxi-driver growled, 'Wot a night!' as she fumbled in her purse for change, when she ran coughing up the stairs into the plushy warmth and light and their waiter greeted her with a 'Good evening, Mrs. Craven. Mr. Craven's waiting at your table. I'll bring along your sherries right away.'

She would go over to their table, sit down, and slide her hand palm upwards along the sofa seat until his hand closed round it.

'Good evening, Mrs. Craven,' he would say, and they would both laugh.

They always enjoyed the joke that the waiter supposed they were married. It went with the respectability of Porter's that any nice couple who dined together continuously over a long period of time should be thought of as husband and wife. 'We're one in the sight of God and Mrs. Siddons,' he said, but although she laughed, it wasn't a joke with her. She liked being called Mrs. Craven. It gave her a warm feeling round the heart, because she could pretend for a moment that things were different and that he had no wife and three fine children who would be broken in bits by a divorce. He had long ago made her see the sense of this, and now she was careful never to make scenes or to sound the demanding note

which he hated. Her value for him was to be always there, calm and understanding. 'You smooth me out,' he said sometimes. 'You give me more peace than anyone in the world.' She was a wonderful listener. She would sit watching him with a little smile while he told her all the details of his week. He often talked about the children. At her flat, standing in front of the mirror tying his tie, he would tell her proudly how clever eight-year-old Jennifer was, or how well Pete was coming on at school. On these occasions the little smile sometimes grew a trifle rigid on her lips.

They never went anywhere but Porter's. In a queer sort of way, although he was known by name, he seemed to feel safe and anonymous there. 'None of the people one knows comes here,' he said, by which he meant none of the people his wife knew. More men than women ate at Porter's. Very occasionally he was greeted by a business acquaintance, who would nod and call across the room, 'How are you?' Then he would call back heartily, 'Fine! How are *you*?' but he would be a little uncomfortable all through the meal. If she slid her hand towards his knee, he would pretend not to notice, and he would talk in a brisk, cheerful way which, at a distance, might look like the kind of manner one would use when dining with a female cousin up from the country or a secretary one had kept working late and taken along for some food out of sheer good nature.

Sometimes she felt that she would like to put on a low-cut gown and go somewhere where there were lights and dancing, where she could walk in proudly, with him following her without taking a swift, surreptitious look round the room first

to see who was there. But she knew how worried he would look if she suggested it, how he would say, 'Darling, I wish we could, but you know it's impossible. Someone would be sure to spot us. We've got to be careful – haven't we?' By now she had learned exactly how to dress for their Thursday evenings. The clothes had to make her look beautiful for him, but they must be on the unadventurous side so that no one would cast an interested remembering glance from an opposite table. She often wore brown, and sometimes she had a funny feeling that she was invisible against the brown wall and the faded prints of the Prince of Denmark and the noblest Roman of them all.

When the war came, he got a commission in a mechanised regiment. Their Thursday evenings were interrupted, and when he got home on leave things were often difficult. There was a family dinner party, or the children were back from school. 'You know how it is, darling,' he would say ruefully on the telephone. But every now and then he sent her a telegram and came dashing up to London for a few hours. Porter's still looked the same except that most of the men were in uniform, and the old waiter always saw to it that they got their usual table. 'Good evening, Mrs. Craven,' he would say shambling forward when he saw her. 'You're expecting Mr. Craven? . . . Ah, that's fine. The pigeon casserole is just how he likes it today.'

They dined together just before he went to Libya. There were two men drinking port at the next table, one with white hair and beautiful, long hands who looked like a Galsworthy family lawyer, the other round and red.

'Don't think I'm being stupid and morbid,' she said, 'but supposing anything happens. I've been worrying about that. You might be wounded or ill and I wouldn't know.' She tried to laugh. 'The War Office doesn't have a service for sending telegrams to mistresses, does it?'

He frowned, because this sounded hysterical, and glanced sharply at the old men at the next table, who went right on drinking port and talking in their tired old voices.

'Darling,' he said, 'don't start getting ideas like that into your head. If anything did happen – but it won't – I'd get someone to let you know right away.'

She had a wild impulse to ask him how this would be possible when he would be lying broken and bloody, alone in the sand. With an effort, she remembered that he loved her because she was calm, because she was not the kind of woman to make scenes or let the tears run down her face in public.

'I know you would,' she said. 'Don't worry about me. Remember, dearest, you don't have to worry about me one little bit.'

'Good night, Mrs. Craven. Good night, Mr. Craven,' said the old waiter, hurrying after them as they went out.

A long time after he left, his letters began to arrive. They were not very satisfactory. He wrote in the same hearty style that he put on at Porter's for the business acquaintances' benefit, and she had the feeling he was worried the censor might turn out to be his wife's second cousin. She worked hard at a war job and lost a lot of weight. The girl who washed her hair said, 'My goodness, aren't you getting grey!' and she longed foolishly to be able to tell her about it and get her sympathy. There was no one to confide in; all these years she had been so careful that she had hardly mentioned his name to anyone else. She went out with other people, but she imagined that she wasn't so amusing or attractive as she used to be and that they noticed it. She began to stay home most evenings, reading in bed or writing him long letters. Before he left, they had settled on various little code words which would give her an idea of where he was, so she was able to tell when he was up in the front lines or when he had gone back to Cairo for leave.

After a while his letters stopped, but she wasn't seriously worried at first. She knew that the mails were often bad; there had been long gaps before. But this time hard fighting was going on in Libya, and she had a terrible premonition that something had happened. She found that she could hardly sleep at all, and when she came home in the evenings, her hand shook as she put the key in the door. She made herself take the letters out of the box and look through them very slowly. Afterwards she would go into the living-room, sit down, and stare blankly out of the window at the barrage balloons glittering in the late sunlight.

One evening she came in after a hard day's work, and as she stood getting the key out of her purse, she knew that there would be a letter or a cable waiting for her. She was so positive of it that she was tremulous with relief as she got the door open and stooped to the mailbox. There was nothing except a bill for a repair to the radio set. She stood, feeling cold and stupid, then she went swiftly to the living-room telephone and looked up a number in the book. As she dialled it and then listened to the bell buzzing, it seemed odd to her to think how many times he must have heard it ring through that unknown house.

When a child's voice, high, and carefully a little overloud, answered, she was slightly taken aback. She said, 'Is this Mrs. Craven's house?' The child's voice said, 'Yes. This is Jennifer. Do you want Mummy? . . . I'll get her.'

After a pause she heard footsteps on a hardwood floor, and then a new voice said, 'Hello? Yes?'

She had thought out what to say, and she made her voice crisp and friendly.

'Good evening, Mrs. Craven,' she said. 'I do want to apologise for troubling you like this. You won't know my name, but I'm an old friend of Mr. Craven's, and I've only just heard that he's in Libya. I thought I'd like to ring up and see if you've had good news of him.'

'Why, that's nice of you,' Mrs. Craven said pleasantly. 'To tell you the truth, I've heard nothing very recently, but I try not to worry. He'll cable me when he has a minute. Judging by the papers, I shouldn't think any of them have a minute.'

'No, I don't suppose they have,' she said. She could hear the little girl calling out, as if to a dog. She knew that there were two dogs, and that there was French Empire furniture in the room, and on the mantelpiece stood a little Chinese figure in white porcelain with a scroll in its hand. She had helped choose it one Christmas. Mrs. Craven sounded calm and unfussed. She could picture her standing at the telephone, smiling slightly, secure in the middle of her own familiar things, maybe watching the child abstractedly out of the corner of her eye while she dealt courteously with this well-meaning stranger.

The pleasant voice said, 'Luckily, I'm tremendously busy myself. That helps to keep one's mind off things, doesn't it? I'm so sorry, I don't think I quite caught the name.'

She mumbled a name that might have been anything and added lightly, 'Just someone Mr. Craven used to know a long while ago. Goodbye, Mrs. Craven, and thanks so much. I hope you hear good news very soon.'

She hung up the receiver and sat for a long time without moving. Then she began to weep bitterly. The tears poured down her face, and she rocked her body backward and forward. 'I can't go on,' she sobbed, as though he were there in the room with her. 'I can't, can't go on. You'll have to break them up – I don't care. I just can't go on this way any longer.' She thought of his wife sitting in their home on the other side of town, and the contrast seemed too bitter to bear. All those years of Thursday evenings seemed like a pathetic game of make-believe – two children playing at housekeeping in a playhouse with three walls. After a while she grew quieter. She sat thinking of him, wondering whether, wherever he was, he would have had a sense of something breaking sharply in two, coming apart with a hum, like a snapped wire. Already she could feel the relaxed tension, as though whatever had been holding her taut all these years had suddenly gone limp.

Tomorrow she would write and tell him, but not now. She couldn't remember when she had felt so tired. She went into the bathroom to bathe her face, and then came back and began taking off her dress. There was a brooch pinned at the neck, and she undid it and stood looking at it for a moment. It was a discreetly beautiful thing of dark, old garnets – diamonds, he had pointed out, were too likely to cause comment, and didn't suit her, either. She put down the brooch and finished undressing. Maybe, she thought, she would wait until after tomorrow to write to him, for she had a feeling that tomorrow there would be a letter from him. She was sure of it. She could see it lying in the mailbox, addressed in that small, neat, familiar hand. If it wasn't there tomorrow, it would be there the next day. She would go to Porter's for dinner, sit at their table, and read it over and over. 'Good news from Mr. Craven, Mrs. Craven?' the old waiter would say as he leaned protectively over her. 'Ah, that's fine, that's fine.'

She began to smile, but suddenly she closed her eyes for a minute. She had had a queer sensation of falling, of the room slipping away and of herself falling, falling, as one does in a dream, without being able to stop and without wondering or caring what lies at the bottom.

THE HUNGER OF MISS BURTON

16th January 1943

Ever since food began to get a bit tight, Miss Burton had carried a wolf around with her under the neat waistband of her tweed skirt. Sometimes she felt that it wasn't one wolf only. It was a whole wolf pack cutting up in the vacuum at the back of her grey herringbone. Before the war, she couldn't remember thinking much about food, but now she thought about it constantly. She thought of thick steaks sitting on beds of fried onions, of cakes topped with a Mont Blanc of whipped cream, of black cherry jam on hot, flaky *croissants*. Now and then she even dreamed about them, as in the old days she used to dream about love. No more erotic visions of unknown or (even more embarrassing) known males flitted disturbingly through Miss Burton's slumbers. Instead, they were punctuated with good blowouts of dream food which never had any taste, which melted tantalisingly into the slow return of the chilly room and the school bell clamorously ringing.

Miss Burton's wolves were at their worst in the middle of the morning, just before break. Then they leaped about playfully, producing awkward rumbling noises which must, she often felt, be audible to Mr. Duval, romping through *'falloir'* with the Second Form next door. Sometimes she glanced sharply at the boys, expecting to catch them grinning. But they were too preoccupied with their own hunger, poor little devils, counting the moments until their eleven o'clock glass of milk and a biscuit. The staff let up also for cups of tea in the staff room – old Blenkinsop, little bald Kendall, Duval with his stiff leg. All the young masters had gone by now; there was no one to flirt with, even if one felt inclined. Miss Burton seldom felt inclined any longer. Probably food was at the back of that, too; sex impulses don't flourish on a meagre diet. Her one glorious flutter, the affair with Emil that walking summer holiday in the Black Forest, had been done on rich, stupefying food – garlic sausage, pig's knuckle and buttery cabbage, enormous draughts of beer. Emil was dead now, his country was at war with hers, that innocent Germany had vanished like a dream into the forest. Lately she hadn't even bothered to have the grey in her hair touched up to a dark, unreal-looking auburn.

When she went along to the staff room one Saturday morning towards the end of the autumn term, she found Kendall and the others already there, standing warming their hands round their cups of tea as though they were holding small individual braziers. They were being economical on the central heating this year, and in the staff-room grate smouldered a few dejected logs to which Mrs. Baker, the headmaster's wife, always referred as 'a jolly wood fire'. When Miss Burton came in, Kendall was puffing at it unhopefully with the bellows, and Margaret Pierce, the music mistress, was saying, 'I'm famished as well as frozen. Breakfast this

morning was really too ludicrous – some of the mothers are going to start complaining before you can say knife.' Miss Burton poured herself a cup of tea and gulped the hot liquid gratefully, feeling it cut the classroom chill in her insides. 'It's something about this wartime food,' she said. 'I eat and eat bread, but I get up feeling that I haven't had anything.' 'Well, thank God I haven't got much more of it,' said Margaret. She was leaving at the end of the term to marry a Canadian soldier named Jay Sturges, whom she had met at a local dance. Miss Burton stared at her, standing warming her long, slender legs in front of Mrs. Baker's jolly wood fire, and snapped, 'If I were ten years younger, my child, you wouldn't catch me stopping here one moment longer than was necessary, either.' Margaret just yawned and nodded unbelievingly, hitching her skirt a little higher at the back so that Kendall had a good view of the silk stockings Jay had given her. 'How long till lunch, oh Lord, how long?' she sighed as Miss Burton picked up her books and went out.

When the morning eventually ended and the lunch for which Margaret had prayed arrived, it turned out to be of the variety which looks ample but soon subsides, leaving a vacuum. Miss Burton, who presided over one of the tables, wondered how many more ways Miss Ruddock, the hard-pressed cook, would think up of disguising vegetables as something else. And pulse! Really, with the amount of pulse that was stuffed into the boys, the poor little wretches' insides must be blown out with enough wind to start an Atlantic gale. It was a temptation to give herself a slightly larger helping of the hot treacle roly-poly – after all, the boys had mothers who sent them things, potted meat and jam; Morley, the urchin on her right, had had a cake as big as his head this week – but she was scrupulously fair down to the last crumb.

As she began to eat, careful not to bolt the delicious sweet stuff for which she was pining, she remembered thankfully that it was Saturday and her turn to be off duty. Usually she went into the town with Margaret Pierce or Miss Ruddock, and they shopped and went to a film. It wasn't particularly exciting, but there was a bogus Elizabethan café in the High Street where they served hot chocolate and really nice homemade scones. Miss Burton enjoyed sitting in a corner under the orange-shaded wrought-iron candelabra, glancing through an old *Tatler* and feeling the warmth of the shopping women at the tables all round her, with their flushed, homely faces and their baskets full of food. It was something, at any rate, to get away from St. Ermin's for an hour or two.

But Margaret, buttonholed as they were all pouring out of the dining-room, shook her head.

'Sorry, Burty,' she said, 'I can't manage a flick today. I've got a date.'

'I suppose it's Jay,' said Miss Burton.

'We're going to a dance at the Red Lion this evening. See you on the bus, though.'

As they trundled towards the market town later that afternoon, separated by countrywomen with bundles and soldiers with rifles and packs, Miss Burton glanced at

Margaret across the bus and reflected grudgingly that she was looking nice. She was wearing her good blue coat, and the scarf twisted round her red hair brought out the colour of her eyes. Although she wasn't a type which would have appealed to Emil – Emil had liked women to be cosily built – most men would think her attractive. It was obvious that some man, Jay Sturges or another, would want to take her away from pounding out Czerny's Piano Exercises with stupid kids who hadn't a spark of music in their souls. As always on the days when she was meeting Jay, she had a bright, happy expression of anticipation, different from the fretful look she wore all week at St. Ermin's. Miss Burton had a sudden horrid pang of envy, an empty, dropping sensation worse than anything experienced in those moments when her wolves were clamouring.

'Well, have a good time,' she said when the bus rattled into the market place and they all got out.

'Be good!' Margaret called gaily, and hurried off through the crowd.

More leisurely, Miss Burton progressed up the packed High Street, with stops at some of the shop windows, in which she saw herself reflected, portrait of a gentlewoman in grey herringbone with a party of wolves under the third button. As she suspected, lunch had subsided and she was ravening again, but there was a little time to be filled in before she could decently make tracks for Ye Olde Tudor Café. She entered a sweetshop and bought her week's ration of chocolate. At least, it was better now that it was rationed. You could be sure of getting it, and not have some hateful, pert girl snap, 'Any children? We keep it for the children now,' with her hand resting beside the pile of little twopenny bars and her impudent, mocking eyes searching Miss Burton's face as though expecting to see marriage lines there in electric lights. Coming out, she was halted by the sight of a mound of freshly boiled lobsters in the fishmonger's. One holiday before the war, the parents of one of the boys, wealthy people named Douglas, had asked her out to lunch in London, and they had had lobster salad at Scott's – an ambrosial lobster with thick mayonnaise, followed by raspberries and cream, coffee, and a Cointreau that sent Miss Burton walking on air out into Piccadilly, telling Mr. Douglas that his son was the sort of boy who every once in a while made the teaching profession seem worth while. He had been charming, she remembered. Well, she had still taken trouble over how she looked in those days, before she became merely a disembodied stomach with a menagerie prowling about in it. Now, nothing seemed important any more compared with the small, private sensuality of eating.

The memory had made her mouth water, and she crossed the road quickly to the orange-shaded warmth of Ye Olde Tudor Café. She sat there for an hour or more, spinning out her order of hot chocolate and scones, glancing ironically at the pictures of well-fed people in the *Tatler*. 'The Lady Marigold Taggart-Bly leads an austere life at her cottage in the country.' A week at St. Ermin's, my girl, and you'd know all about austerity. Soldiers and their girls came in, the men clumping a bit self-consciously, the girls with rosy, shining faces

under their pert hats. Miss Burton wondered suddenly what Margaret and Jay were doing. She asked for a second order of scones, and ate them to the last crumb with deliberate, enjoyable greed.

At the cinema, she saw the feature picture through and then sat on for a bit of the beginning again. It was comfortably warm in there, and the star was a big, fair fellow who reminded her of Emil. If he were alive now, he would be forty-eight and her enemy, but she saw him always as a young man of twenty-seven, wearing a comic green hat and leather pants and looking as beautiful as a god. All round her, couples were nuzzling and making unabashed love as they watched the picture. Maybe Margaret was there, sitting happily in the darkness, feeling a man's cheek against her hair as she pretended to watch that nonsense on the screen. Miss Burton felt tired and depressed all at once, and suspected that she had a headache coming.

She was early for the bus, after all. She sat in the little shelter, squeezed up on a bench next to a stout woman and her tired, wailing children. The winter evening was still and beautiful, and there was a wonderful full moon. Miss Burton was wondering what there would be for supper – on Saturday evenings Miss Ruddock sometimes spread herself a little – and debating whether she should open her packet of chocolate or not, when she saw Margaret and Jay on the opposite side of the market place. She was surprised, for Margaret had said that she was coming home on the last bus, and she watched them curiously as they walked up and down in the moonlight. Jay was very tall; she would have known him anywhere by his height. He and Margaret stopped, still talking. Then they went on again, but a few yards further on they stopped for the second time, and suddenly Jay turned on his heel and walked off, and Margaret came hurrying over to the shelter.

'Halloa!' said Miss Burton. 'I thought you and Jay were going to make a night of it.'

'We changed our minds,' said Margaret shortly.

Before Miss Burton could say any more, the bus came in and they had to scramble for seats. It was dark inside the bus, the lights were partly blacked over, and everyone's face looked greenish and ghostly. Miss Burton decided against opening the chocolate now, for it would be difficult to avoid offering Margaret a piece.

'Did you go to the cinema?' she asked.

Margaret didn't answer, and Miss Burton, with a little shock, realised that she was crying. She was sitting, swaying with the movement of the bus, and the tears were running down her face and dropping on the blue coat. Miss Burton thought, 'They've quarrelled, he's let her down,' and through her mind flashed the idea that they might have broken the engagement. The chocolate slid off her lap, and she bent mechanically to pick it up. She didn't feel like opening it, now. The Olde Tudor tea must have been more filling than she realised, for she felt a sense of utter, wonderful repletion, as though she had just had a satisfying meal that would last a long time.

'Two to the St. Ermin's gates,' she said to the bus

conductress, in such a strong, buoyant tone that the other people turned their greenish faces towards her in dim astonishment.

IT'S THE REACTION

24 July 1943

∽∾∾∾∾∾∾∾∾∾∾

Miss Catherine Birch trotted through the lobby of the ministry where she was employed, automatically waved her pass at the doorman, and joined the hurrying throng of men and women pouring down the London street towards the bus stops and tube stations. Their haste was contagious. She began to scurry along as though a vitally important evening lay before her. Most of the other female employees of the ministry were girls with hatless manes of long, glossy hair hanging round their shoulders or setted up in red or blue snoods. The evening was warm, and they raced along bare-legged in their flimsy sandals, their bright, cheap coats hanging open. In contrast, Miss Birch seemed to be wearing a great many clothes. Her tailored suit, felt hat, Liberty-silk scarf, stockings, gloves, chubby, rolled umbrella, briefcase, and sensible morocco-grained leather bag gave her something of the appearance of a schoolmistress bringing up the rear of a double column of dryads.

In the tube, the ministry faces thinned out and merged with greater London. Miss Birch stood in the packed train with her near-morocco purse pressed against the bosom of a stout matron in slacks, while her hatbrim brushed the cheek of a young American soldier who was despairingly studying the map of stations over their heads. Her mind went on fretting over that morning's row in the department. She didn't really know how it had happened. She had felt tired and out of sorts, someone's stupid inaccuracy had inflamed her, and the next thing she knew, she was having it out with Mr. Danvers. After the row was over, her hands shook and her voice was weak and quavery. She went to the women's washroom before lunch, wishing that she could lock herself in and have a good howl. Nan Cruddock, from the department, was there, powdering her nose and drawing a modish square mouth over the Victorian bow with which nature had afflicted her. 'Know what I think, Birch?' Nan had said kindly as she leaned towards the mirror, while alongside her Miss Birch dabbed her cheeks with a leaf torn from a little book of *papier poudre*. 'Know what? It's about time you had some leave. Ask Danvers for some, go off down to the country and find a cow to look at, and for God's sake relax. If you don't, you're for the ministry heebie-jeebies – in plain English, darling, a breakdown. Heavens, I must fly!' And she had rushed off to lunch with the usual mob of people. She was a good-hearted creature, though, in spite of her flightiness, and there might even be some common sense in what she said, Miss Birch had reflected later over her solitary sandwich in the canteen. Maybe things had been working up to the morning's flare-up for quite a while.

The train filled and emptied, the American boy got out, and Miss Birch leaned against other bosoms before she got to her own station. It was ten minutes' walk from there to Richelieu House, the block of flats where she lived. Three or four of the neighbourhood shops were still open; this district

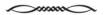

resembled a village, flowing on in its muddled eighteenth-century way round the twentieth-century blocks of steel and concrete which had grown up in it. Miss Birch called in at the little tobacconist-newsagent on the corner by the public house and bought some cigarettes. The woman behind the counter said, 'I've got your Player's this evening, but only loose – no packets. Will that do?'

Miss Birch said that it would. Tucking the chubby umbrella under one arm and digging down for change, she had a sudden sociable impulse to start up a little conversation, to say something which would keep her standing there in the shop, sniffing the smell of frying that was coming out of the back room. She said in a friendly voice, 'My goodness, how your plant has grown! It's really a beauty now,' nodding towards a potted cactus which stood on a table next to a sleeping ginger cat. The woman glanced at it and said, 'Yes, it's doing well, isn't it?' Miss Birch picked up her handful of cigarettes and went out. The impulse hadn't come to anything after all. If it had been Nan Cruddock, now, she knew perfectly well that with half a dozen words Nan would have leaned over the counter and dragged that woman into her life. With a roll of those round blue eyes, she would have built up something warm and friendly in no time. It was years now that Miss Birch had been calling in for her cigarettes and never getting much beyond a 'good evening'. Never, that is, except when the blitz was on and everything was different.

Miss Birch went on thinking about the blitz as she walked to her own block and went up in the lift with a Mr. Masters, who lived on the same floor.

'Evening,' he said pleasantly. 'Having a lovely bit of weather, aren't we?'

'Lovely,' said Miss Birch.

Mr. Masters let himself into his flat which was close to the lift, and Miss Birch walked on down the passage, fumbling for her key. Behind the little black doors she could hear people talking on the telephone, playing their radios, running their bath water. No doubt all the other tenants on Floor K could hear, if they chose to listen, her footsteps ringing out now down the passageway. When she left, early in the morning, milk bottles stood outside the doors with newspapers folded on top of them. The neat, sealed bottles were like footprints discovered on the floor of an ancient cliff city, a sign that life existed somewhere in this echoing honeycomb. Except for the laughter behind the black doors and the occasional chance encounters in the lift, Miss Birch might have fancied herself alone in Richelieu House.

She opened her door, and, crossing to the window, jerked up the blind which she had prudently lowered before leaving so that the afternoon sun would not take the colour out of the blue divan cover and matching armchair. With all those pretty Chinese cushions, a guest would never have suspected that the divan was Miss Birch's bed until, seating himself, his knees flew up and hit him on the chin. There was a small gateleg table at which she had her meals, sitting upright on a blue chair. Black-framed Medici prints, reproductions of old Italian masters, hung in an even row on the distempered cream wall above the bookcase. In the opposite wall were doors leading to a box of a bathroom and a cupboard of a kitchenette.

Miss Birch remained for a few minutes at the window, still grasping umbrella and briefcase, absently watching the barrage balloons lolling over London. They fitted in with her train of thought. She could remember when they didn't look like absurd silver Jumbos browsing in space but when she had thought of them as guardians and felt consoled because they were there. By leaning to the right and twitching the net curtain aside, she could see down into the street where, five minutes or so earlier, she had been buying her cigarettes. Seen from above, the jagged space where a bomb had fallen just behind the public house was more noticeable than it was from the road, now that they had cleared the debris away. A land mine had come down, too, not far away. After that awful night, the woman at the tobacconist's had taken Miss Birch into the back parlour to show her the broken windows and the rubble dust lying thick over everything. 'It's a wonder the whole place didn't come down, and that's a fact,' she had said, fetching a packet of cigarettes up from under the counter and shoving them over to Miss Birch.

'Here you are, dear. Pop 'em in your bag. They're short, but if we don't get our smokes to quiet our nerves we'll all go balmy, more than likely.'

Miss Birch left the window and began taking off her outdoor things, noting that the evening looked settled enough to warrant leaving the chubby umbrella at home tomorrow. She hung her suit carefully on a hanger and changed into an old print summer dress which she kept for wearing at home. After that she usually laid the table for supper. When it was over, she would wash up, perhaps glance over the report she

had brought home with her, mend a pair of stockings, and go to bed early with a book. It was her usual way of spending a nice quiet evening, but this evening, for some reason, she didn't feel like setting it in motion right away. Her head ached badly, probably the result of this morning's row. She went into the bathroom and took a couple of aspirins. Then she came back and sat down in the armchair by the window.

The details of the office upset flitted through her mind again, but only for a moment. Footsteps sounded outside in the corridor, a door banged, and several people seemed to be laughing and talking together. Miss Birch heard a woman's voice saying emphatically, 'But if we didn't phone we'll *never* get a table.' The pint milk bottle at Flat 6, just across the passage, must have had a party, which was now proceeding out en masse to find some dinner. At one time the occupants of Flat 6 had meant rather more than a milk bottle in Miss Birch's life. They were a Mr. and Mrs. Chalmers, and night after night in the blitz they had unrolled their mattresses alongside Miss Birch's mattress in the corridor on Floor B. Miss Birch, over a shared thermos of tea, had learned that Mrs. Chalmers had married when she was eighteen and that Mr. Chalmers was allergic to cats. She came to know by heart such small, intimate details as the colour of their pyjamas, the smell of Mrs. Chalmers' face cream. And early in the morning, just before the all-clear sounded jubilantly over battered London, Mr. Chalmers would begin to snore.

Those nights, terrible as they had been, certainly had had their compensations. It seemed to Miss Birch, looking back, that the inhabitants of Floor K had been one jolly family,

recognising each other with especial friendliness among all the other prone tenants of Richelieu House. There had been little Mary Rycroft from Flat 2, a pretty child who looked as though she oughtn't to be out alone in a rainstorm, let alone a blitz. There had been Mr. Masters, strolling down the row of mattresses to ask Miss Birch's help with a tough word in *The Times* crossword puzzle or to have a little chat about books. One evening he had noticed that she was reading *Nicholas Nickleby*, and the next evening he had ambled along to say that he had taken her advice and was starting on his tenth reading of *Pickwick Papers* that very night. 'You're right, Miss Birch,' he had said. 'There's nothing like the old fellows for keeping one's mind off the fellows up there,' and he had nodded towards the racket overhead. 'Pickwick seems to make 'em unimportant, somehow.' They had got really close, like old friends in those talks in the stuffy corridor, listening subconsciously for the warning scream, the sudden hole in the air, the slow glacier of bricks and mortar slipping into the street below. Now he was only a man who took off his hat politely in the lift and said 'Evening' before fumbling for his key, going in, and shutting his front door.

Little by little, as normality came back and the passages of Richelieu House were no longer filled with flitting figures carrying torches and pillows, the sense of being neighbours had worn off. Mrs. Chalmers, if she and Miss Birch met in the lift, said, 'Do you know, I've been meaning and *meaning* to ring you,' and at the back of her worried baby eyes and plucked eyebrows, Miss Birch could see the thought forming that one of these days they must really ask the old girl over, fill her up with gin, do something about it. After a while, even that thought disappeared. Mrs. Chalmers simply said 'Hello' and smiled vaguely, as though Miss Birch were someone she had once met at a party.

Sitting in the blue armchair, the headache nagging at her, Miss Birch wondered if it wasn't partly her own fault. Maybe there was something she could have said or done, some magic password which would have kept that wonderful new friendliness going. If she hadn't frightened them off, Mary Rycroft or Mr. Masters might have been dropping in for a chat this evening. She pictured Mr. Masters saying in his breezy way 'This is something like!' as she brought out the beer that she would make a point of keeping in the refrigerator for him. While he drank it, leaning back against the Chinese cushions and flicking his cigarette ash, manlike, over her blue rug, she would tell him about this morning's dust-up with Danvers. Telling it to him, getting his calm, man's point of view, would be a relief far greater than the good howl she had promised herself all day. He would say, 'Don't worry, my dear girl, it's nothing,' and sure enough it would be nothing. Then he would get up, glass in hand, and wander over to the bookcase. 'I might have known that you'd be the woman to read William Blake,' he would say cosily.

With sudden determination, Miss Birch stood up. She peeped in the mirror, patted a few stray wisps of hair into place, and gave a nervous twitch to the neck of her dress. Then, looking in her bag to make sure that her key was there, she opened the door of her apartment, closed it behind her, and began walking rapidly down the passage towards the lift.

Mr. Masters' electric bell had a different note from hers, she noticed. It sounded loud and startled, and Mr. Masters also looked startled when he answered it. 'Why – come in!' he said after the faintest possible pause. Her picture of him had been correct, insofar as he was holding a bottle of beer and an opener in his free hand. He was in his shirtsleeves, and when she walked past him into a frowsier version of her own room, she noticed that his tie was lying on the table with the evening paper, some gramophone records, and a bowl of ice cubes. He made a lunge towards it, and she said, 'Oh, please don't bother to get smartened up for me! It's quite warm this evening, isn't it?'

'Feels to me as though we're going to get a bit of thunder,' he said. 'Sit down, won't you? I was just . . . ' and he made an embarrassed gesture with the beer bottle and the opener.

'Do go on,' said Miss Birch. 'I do hope you don't mind my dropping in informally like this. As a matter of fact, I haven't a thing to read, and I wondered if you'd very kindly lend me a book.'

It sounded prim to her own ears, like something she might have written on a memo form in the office. Mr. Masters stopped looking nonplussed and, setting down the beer, gestured to the row of untidy bookshelves against the wall corresponding to the one where Miss Birch's Medici prints hung. 'Help yourself,' he said. 'I don't know that you'll find anything much there, but you're welcome.'

She came forward and made a pretence of looking at the titles. Smiling up at him, she said, 'You know, I always think of you as a bookish sort of person. Remember our talks

about Dickens and Thackeray and Trollope in the old blitz days.'

The information that she had thought about him at all brought Mr. Masters' surprised expression back again. 'Oh, those,' he said uneasily. 'Well, thank God that time's a long way back now. Seems like a nightmare, doesn't it? I don't believe we'll ever get 'em coming over like that again, either.'

'Oh, I hope not,' said Miss Birch.

With lightning, cruel clarity she knew that the visit wasn't going to come off. Nan would have been sitting down within two minutes in the one armchair in the place, crossing her legs above the knee, sharing Mr. Masters' beer, smoking his cigarettes, roaring with laughter at jokes that wouldn't be bookish quips about Trollope and Thackeray. Miss Birch, peering blindly along the shelves, was tongue-tied. She pulled out a volume without even bothering to look at its title and straightened up. 'Might I borrow this?' she asked. There didn't seem to be much more to say. Mr. Masters became heartier and obviously a good deal relieved as he accompanied her to the door. 'Any time you want to borrow another, just pop along,' he said.

Miss Birch's room seemed very still in the evening sunlight as she let herself in. She walked over to the window and stood looking out again at the silver blimps floating aimlessly against the sky. London looked beautiful in this clear light, calm and radiant, as though its sirens would never sound again this side of the grave. Listening to that implacable silence, Miss Birch felt the delayed tears stinging at the back

of her throat and nose. 'It's the reaction,' she said aloud, as though she were defending herself to someone. 'You can't go through month after month of that and not get a reaction sometime.' She dropped Mr. Masters' book into the chair and became suddenly busy, laying the checked cloth on the gateleg table and putting the milk for her cup of Ovaltine on to boil. It was going to be another nice quiet evening after all, she thought hopelessly.

CUT DOWN THE TREES

4 September 1943

⌒◦◦◦◦◦◦⌒

The old lady, Mrs. Walsingham, lived alone in the big house by the river with her maid, old Dossie. Alone, that is to say, except for forty Canadian soldiers who had taken over most of the house, parked their trucks in the lime avenue, and built their huts on the damp English meadows sloping down to the slow, heron-haunted English stream. Mrs. Walsingham had kept for her own use her room and Dossie's, an extra one for guests, the dining-room, and the library. The drawing-room was under Holland covers, because Dossie and Mrs. Bunt, who came up from the lodge occasionally to lend a hand, could not be expected to keep it dusted and polished too. Dossie had mourned as they packed away the crystal chandeliers and hung dust sheets over the Gainsborough and the Zoffany conversation pieces, but Mrs. Walsingham had been firm.

'There's already more than you and I can do here,' she said, 'and the days of sitting in drawing-rooms are over, for the moment, anyway. We're all too busy.'

'If we could get a couple of housemaids from the village, that would be something,' said Dossie sourly. 'But there are no girls left. They're all in the Waafs or something like that, larking about, getting into mischief with their bobbed heads and their lipstick and all. They'll want sobering down before anyone will take them into good private service after the war, Madam, and no mistake.'

Mrs. Walsingham laughed and limped over to close an emptied Queen Anne cabinet, her stick tapping with a hollow sound on the bare, polished floor. 'Maybe they won't want to be taken,' she said. 'Until they do, you and I will have to crawl round as best we can, Dossie. That's the last packing case. Boxall can come in and take it down to the cellars.'

Dossie, still unconvinced, said, 'Yes, Madam. But if we did get a couple of girls – young ones who wouldn't be called up yet – if we did, it wouldn't be a bit of good with all those soldiers about. You know what happened to Mavis.'

'Well,' said Mrs. Walsingham briskly, 'it's not a bad thing, with the birth rate the way it is. They're fine young men, the Canadians. You don't want England populated with nothing but old crocks like you and me, do you?'

Dossie sniffed but did not answer. Mrs. Walsingham had behaved with regrettable airiness over the affair of Mavis, the last kitchen maid who had flitted through the big house in the days when the kitchen still had a cook in it. For Mavis, unrepentant and blooming after fatal evening strolls along the river with a corporal from Vancouver, Mrs. Walsingham had managed to find one of those layettes from America with two of everything, one pink, one blue. She had also provided a pram and sent the girl grapes from the hothouses. Not that it was entirely Mavis's fault, Dossie thought, though it was true that Mavis had gone on her unfortunate expeditions

under the willows not with the air of a lamb being led to the slaughter but rather with the spryness of a young pussycat slipping off down the garden. No, it was those men, those soldiers who were to blame for everything.

Dossie had never had any use for the Canadians from the day they came. Of course, it wasn't precisely their fault that they were there, but it made her sick to hear their big boots clattering up and down the stairs and to see their trucks standing in line along the lime avenue. When she came across a bunch of them messing about, their heads deep in the bonnets of their trucks, she would either hurry past with averted eyes or say primly, 'Good afternoon,' and jerk her head in a brief grudging salutation. Sloppy, she would say to herself as she went by, sloppy young chaps in those nasty khaki romper affairs, no spit and polish, nothing smart and military about them at all. They would watch her walking towards them and their heads would slowly swivel to watch her out of sight, with the marooned male's desperate interest in a skirt, even though the neat navy-blue article in question covered the limbs of Miss Dossie, the old girl at the big house. The more audacious would whistle and shout 'Hiya, Miss Dossie!' or even 'Hiya, sweetheart!', grinning and wiping the engine oil off their hands along the seat of their pants. Friendly as puppies, they seemed to interpret Dossie's outraged glare as that fine old British reserve that you read about in books. Now and then she attempted to put one right. One day a sunburnt blond youngster, coming round to the kitchen on some errand, said cheerfully, 'Say, your Mrs. Walsingham is

certainly a grand old guy. We think she's swell, the way she stumps around and runs this big old place without any help. Reminds me a lot of my Aunt Katie on the ranch at home.'

Dossie had drawn a deep breath and given him a terse picture of the house as it used to be – shooting parties in the autumn, Mrs. Walsingham in her diamonds at big dinners, and Queen Mary driving over to see the celebrated herbaceous borders when she was staying in the neighbourhood. Interested but un-cowed, the young soldier stood listening. 'Yeah,' he said, 'yeah, Queen Mary. She's another grand old guy.'

If they had called Mrs. Walsingham a grand old guy to her face, Dossie well and disapprovingly knew, her mistress would not have objected. She seemed to like them. Peeping from the house, Dossie would see her limping down towards the home farm with two or three of them in attendance on her, a large imperious old woman in her careless black with a shocking old hat skewer anyhow on her grey hair. Now and then she would pause, with her clothes whipping in the wind, and raise her stick to point out a crop or a prize Guernsey to the young men, who seemed noisily appreciative and not respectfully silent in the uncommunicative island way which Dossie could have understood.

Once a week, their officers, who were billeted elsewhere, came to dine with Mrs. Walsingham. On those evenings, more laughter floated out to Dossie, creaking along the passage with the cheese soufflé and the hot plates trundling on a dinner wagon before her. The dinner wagon was another of Mrs. Walsingham's ideas. 'I can't carry a tray, with my stick, and you'll fall flat on your face if you try,' she had said, 'but we can both push things,' so Dossie thereafter made her entrances in the dining-room as though she were propelling a pram. She had to admit grudgingly, that it was nice to see glass reflected in polished mahogany again, the candles lit, and Mrs. Walsingham leaning back and laughing as serenely as though Jenner and the footman were behind her chair, seeing to dinner, instead of only old Dossie wheezing into the room with her dinner wagon. Yes it was nice, although the Canadian gentlemen couldn't be relied upon not to cry in horribly ringing tones across the table, 'Dossie, you're a pearl among women! This soufflé is even better than the one last week. It's great, isn't it, Mrs. Walsingham?' Bridling with resentment, Dossie would murmur, 'Thank you, sir,' in a voice intended, though failing, to quell some amiable young bear of a major who would be more than likely to bestow on her a cordial hug, its cordiality somewhat heightened by Mrs. Walsingham's Lafitte '24, when she handed him his hat and coat at the end of the evening.

Except for these small hospitable occasions, Mrs. Walsingham had her meals in the kitchen. Observing Dossie's horror the first time she had appeared in the kitchen for a meal, she had said tersely, 'Less way to carry the food. Warmer, too, in the winter. At my age, I'd rather be warm in here than grand in there with a rug over my knees.' So she ate cosily and pleasantly, the heat of the kitchen fire toasting her old back, while Dossie, resisting all invitations to join her, withdrew and chewed morosely in the pantry. She disliked the innovation intensely. It was all part and parcel of the unwarranted bad joke, the conspiracy against Dossie's way of life, which they called a war and which had taken first the menservants and then the girls one by one, which had stopped the central heating, made a jungle of the borders and a pasture of the lawns, marooned the two old women in a gradually decaying house with forty Canadians, and made Mrs. Walsingham stop dressing for dinner.

'It's out of place now,' she had said one day when she came upon Dossie carefully rolling her evening stockings to put out on the bed as usual. 'It's ridiculous for an old woman to dress herself up every night when thousands of young men are being bombed and killed and when thousands more people are starving all over Europe.'

'I'm sure I don't know why a lady shouldn't look nice even if they are,' snapped Dossie.

'Well, if you can't understand that,' said Mrs. Walsingham, 'perhaps you can understand that it's chilly in the evenings without the central heating. I don't want to take things off, my good woman, I want to put them on. If you must put out something, put out my tweed shooting cape.'

Dossie was shocked to the marrow of her being, but there was nothing to be done about it. When peace came, sane existence would be immediately resumed. Dossie sincerely believed that the big house, quietly chipping and mouldering above its meadows, would be instantly repopulated, as though by a genie's wand, with faceless figures in housemaid's print dresses, in dark-blue livery and gardener's baize aprons. She believed that the lawns would be velvet again, that visiting royalty would once more point a gracious umbrella towards

Mrs. Walsingham's Himalayan poppies, that the gentry would know their places and sit over their claret in the dining-room, where they belonged. Dossie had a full and ungrudging faith in the resiliency of the British upper class. Until that day came, she would look after things as much as possible and wait.

Dossie rebelled a little when Colonel Walsingham, Mrs. Walsingham's son, came home from the Middle East on special leave.

'You'll be using the dining-room while the Colonel is with us, I take it, Madam,' she said after he had telephoned that he was in London and would be home in time for dinner.

'Why?' said Mrs. Walsingham wickedly. 'He'll be much more comfortable in the kitchen – always used to like going in there as a little boy, you remember. And I don't suppose he's accustomed to have things very formal in the desert.'

'No, Madam,' said Dossie, going off to set the dining-room table with the scanty silver that hadn't been sent to the bank.

It was the first time Colonel Walsingham had seen his home since the soldiers took over. He walked round and looked at it all quietly and observantly. It was a beautiful August evening and some of the men were playing baseball in one of the meadows. Others were sunbathing after a dip in the river. The smoke from the cookhouse went up thin and straight into the cloudless blue sky and in the house, at one of the upper windows, a soldier was whistling, throwing in an occasional 'Da-da de da'. As the Colonel stood looking down from the terrace, a rabbit came out from behind a group of magnolias and began nibbling away at the long grass on the lawn. It moved confidently, taking no notice of the Colonel, as though it didn't expect to be disturbed.

Dossie had grimly laid out Mrs. Walsingham's black lace dinner dress and set the open jewel cases on the dressing table, so the old lady looked very handsome sitting opposite her son at dinner. He tried not to laugh at the unexpected sight of old Dossie tottering in and out, hanging onto her dinner wagon like an elderly child learning to walk by supporting itself with a toy horse on wheels. 'I had no idea that Dossie could cook,' he said.

'She hadn't either,' said Mrs. Walsingham. 'She's an invaluable creature in lots of ways. Her trouble is that she hates adjusting to the war and she doesn't like me to adjust, either. She has always refused to adjust to anything. I sometimes think that if there's ever a social revolution in England, they'll string Dossie up first before they bother about me.'

Their coffee was waiting for them in the library, where Dossie had been to shake up the sofa cushions and freshly crease *The Times* before ranging it with *The Field* and *The Spectator* on the long velvet stool by the fireplace. This room looks as though nothing had happened, thought the Colonel, strolling over to the window to listen to the distant, nostalgic Canadian singing floating on the quiet air at the back of the house.

'They've cut down some of the trees,' he said.

'They had to, to put up some of their paraphernalia,' said Mrs. Walsingham. 'They were very nice about it. Do you mind,

Edward? To tell you the truth, I think it's an improvement – lets in more light and air. It's altered the view from this side of the house, but what's a view? Everything else is changing so fast I suppose we shouldn't bother about trees and water staying the way they were.'

He nodded, looking out at the gap where the trees had been. He didn't know why that depressed him far more than the latrines dug in the paddock where his pony used to snuffle a hay bag, or the boots clumping on bare boards overhead, or even old Dossie trundling her dinner wagon. After Mrs. Walsingham had gone to bed, he found a stick and called the ecstatic spaniel for a walk round the woods. By the time he got back it was twilight, too dark to notice the huts or the trucks in the drive, and he stood for a moment looking up at the dark shape of the house, which now seemed familiar again, like an old friend sitting against the light so that wrinkles were unnoticeable.

Dossie was lurking in wait for him in the hall.

'The whisky-and-soda are in the library, sir,' she said. 'Do you wish me to call you at eight o'clock, as usual?'

The Colonel opened his mouth to tell her that he didn't want calling, that she should have gone to bed and left him to find the whisky and soda for himself. He closed it again, for he was aware that Dossie was watching him anxiously. The old woman's eyes seemed to implore him to play their game for a little while longer, to pretend that things were just as they used to be, that their world, which had come to an end, could still be saved. And he heard himself answering meekly, dutifully, 'Yes call me at eight, will you, Dossie?'

YEAR OF DECISION

29 April 1944

⟨≈≈≈⟩

Mark Goring sometimes reflected, without bitterness but with rather wry amusement, how he had pictured a war, back in the unbelievable days of peace, and how his own particular war had turned out. The fact couldn't have been more ludicrously different from the fancy. In the first place, he had always somehow imagined himself in the thick of things, living a life which would be quite sharply defined from his peacetime life, dangerous, difficult, and exciting. Nothing of the sort had happened, of course. The fact that he was a specialist in a particular subject had quickly settled him for the duration in a government office, behind an impressively large desk which would doubtless be regarded with a good deal of envy by many other young Englishmen now slogging across Italy. War had differed from peace only in that one worked harder, smoked more, and was progressively more and more uncomfortable at home. But discomfort was hardly danger; except for dodging a few bombs in the blitz, his had been a remarkably safe war. It had taught him none of the stinging, salutary lessons that he had expected. Instead, he had picked up all sorts of curious, unlikely bits of information, such as how to make a bed, scour a greasy saucepan, and lay a

breakfast table so that it did not too greatly resemble the haphazard design of the March Hare's tea party.

It was often a toss-up in Mark's mind as to which was the better thing to do to help Janet – to stay up in London at the club all week or to go back at night to the desirable residence, on a Buckinghamshire common, which they still called home. He could never quite decide whether the charm of his company made up for the trouble he created or whether Janet didn't really prefer to crawl gratefully, after the sort of scratched-up meal which women apparently enjoyed when they were alone, into an early and solitary bed. On the nights he stayed in London, he had to admit guiltily that it was rather pleasant to dine in peace, off china that he wouldn't later have to swab awkwardly with a little mop, and to read luxuriously in a bed which no one expected him to make next morning. Lying there comfortably in a neat room in a club where there was still port in the cellars and help in the kitchen, he would feel bad about Janet, struggling along at home with a biggish house and the dreadful, inescapable fact that the human body needs stoking three times a day. Of course everybody was in the same boat. Servants hardly existed any longer, and it was worse for the old people like his mother, who hadn't a soul to help her in a great barn of a place in Dorset, and four hungry land girls coming in at all hours with their great pink mouths wide open for her to drop hot, satisfying food into. Yes, everybody was in the same boat all right, though it sometimes seemed to Mark that Janet and the rest of their class were making unnecessarily heavy weather of it by refusing to recognise that they were bang in the middle of a social revolution. Life continued in the same old pattern, distorted but recognisable. The Gorings still dined off a polished table, by candlelight, though Mark couldn't help feeling that the sensible thing to do would be to camp in the kitchen. And why not keep the same knife and fork right through dinner, as they made you do in small provincial French restaurants? It would save an astronomical amount of washing up yearly, Mark calculated. But the idea had affronted Janet, who preferred to weep tears of fatigue into the washing-up water. With the helpless obedience and neatness of the performing poodle going through its routine although the rest of the troupe had defaulted, she turned down their bed and laid out her night things, his pyjamas, as they had found them every night of their peacetime married lives. 'For heaven's sake, why bother?' Mark would say. 'It doesn't matter to me or Hitler whether I pick up my pyjamas off a chair or the floor.' But Janet would answer obstinately, 'It matters to me, though,' and go on smoothing the eiderdown, setting her blue mules invitingly, as though the action were yet another moral shot fired at the slowly advancing enemy, as though by setting the mules in their accustomed place she was nailing the brave, idealistic upper-class colours securely for another twenty-four hours.

It was funny, but when he had thought of war back in the good old days, before it had happened, he supposed that he had vaguely pictured Janet seeing him off somewhere, crying down his collar, writing him her particular brand of funny, sweet letter, and waiting for him on an unidentified platform, looking lovely and desirable in a dress he liked. Well, it hadn't

worked out that way. She had seen him off nowhere, she did all her crying into piles of the children's darning after the nine o'clock news, and she seldom looked lovely because she was too busy or tired to care except in sporadic bursts, when she applied a handful of this or that with the cynicism of a witch doctor trying a little juju on a dead woman. 'I'm dead, I'm absolutely dead' had become one of her favorite expressions. War probably hadn't turned out the way she'd expected, either, poor little devil. No doubt she had seen it as a heroic landscape against which she would be gay and courageous, but it had contracted to a strip of floor between stove and sink; the gaiety and courage weren't needed to welcome home a returning warrior in a business suit who had somehow managed to survive the perils of the London rush hour. Maybe it was morbid of him to imagine that she would be happier in a one-room flat somewhere, snatching sandwiches in cafés, and mailing loving air letters to a husband who, thank God, the Army was feeding thousands of miles away.

When they had built the house, it hadn't struck Mark that all its rooms were too big, that the hardwood floors could look like the Sahara to a woman crawling over them with a tin of polish, and that its light paintwork showed up their nice bits of furniture and grubby childish finger marks with equal success. In those days one didn't worry about things like that. Now the house had become an Old Man of the Sea whom, however much he throttled them, they couldn't unseat. If they sold it, they had nowhere to go, and there were Bill and Sally to think of. It was so important for children, said Janet, frantically nailing more of her pathetic little tattered colours to

the mast, to have a secure background, although Mark wasn't certain that getting out from under the feet of a harassed mother all day long was precisely the sort of beautiful, tranquil thing she had in mind. Motherhood was another of Janet's gay and courageous things which in the present hurly-burly, was taking a beating.

Of course he knew perfectly well that he was damned lucky. He and Janet had each other, their home, their children. There were plenty of people who would consider, quite legitimately, that he was having a pleasant and interesting war, for his job was an important one; without even trying to, he was making hundreds of contacts which would be very useful after it was over and he was paddling his own canoe again. It was just that he hadn't pictured himself sitting out Armageddon in an office chair, helping to keep the home fires burning with his sleeves rolled up and one of Janet's aprons tied round his middle. It was funny, that was all.

Going up to London one spring morning, Mark glanced down the *Times* casualty list and saw that a man called Nigel Travers, who had been at school with him, had been killed in action with the Parachute Corps in Italy. Good Lord, old Travers leaping out of planes in parachutes, and he must have been forty or thereabouts, with a nice big wife and some kids, Mark reflected. A quiet, funny sort of devil, too – not the sort of chap you'd have suspected of going out that way. He put the paper down, and began to worry about the hot-water boiler, which hadn't looked too good when he stoked it up before bolting breakfast and dashing for the train. Janet, who had a cold, hadn't looked too good either. One or both of them, he felt, would have given up by the time he got home that night. He picked up the paper again, but the boiler kept on getting between him and the Russians, progress in Italy, poor old Travers plummeting down into some peasant's little bit of vineyard instead of going on, year after undistinguished year, getting in and out of bed with his big, jolly wife.

He wasn't surprised when, later in the morning, Janet rang up to say that she had a temperature and thought it must be flu. A neighbour had charitably come to the rescue and carted off the children for the day, and she was now taking her shivering self to bed. The boiler, Mark was equally unastonished to learn, had gone out. 'Leave it until I get home,' he said with all the cheerfulness he could muster. 'And for God's sake take it easy, darling, and keep warm.'

He bought a paper on the way out to lunch. Life was a perpetual buying of papers, glancing, discarding, as though it were the only way of convincing oneself that the plans over which one slaved day after day, calculating, arguing around tables in close rooms, were somewhere being put into effect by real, living flesh and blood. Another softening-up raid on the French coast, another statesman said that this would be the year of decision, a party of young Norwegians had escaped in a fishing boat. That's the right stuff, thought Mark, that's the right sort of war to be in if you've got to be in one at all. To be twenty-one, sound of wind and limb, shoving off from some dark jetty with your heart banging – yes, that would be all right. Meanwhile, Janet had the flu.

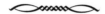

At his club the dining-room was full, mostly of middle-aged, self-confident-looking men leaning alertly forward in discreetly pitched conversations, as though settling the war out of hand between sherry and cigar. Were any of them in jams at home, he wondered. It was hard to picture them in their shirtsleeves at the sink, but maybe it would be equally hard for them to picture him that way. An Air Vice-Marshal across the room nodded at him, and he thought, Has *your* wife got some help, or do you have to get down on your knees in those beautiful trousers, with that chestful of ribbons, and light up the kitchen boiler for her? He started thinking about Travers again. He'd have to hunt up Mrs. Travers' address and write to her, although there was nothing much to say. He didn't know why the thought of Travers, of all people, choosing to get himself killed in that particular way should make him feel faintly irritated, but it did. It seemed so unnecessary, when there were hundreds of safer jobs which he could easily have plumped for. Well, *that* was hardly a line which would make Mrs. Travers feel better.

Back in the office, the incredible thing happened. Mark hadn't finished shaking the spring rain off his hat when his Miss Fletcher said that Arbuthnot would like to see him right away. When he went along, Arbuthnot told him that he was to be sent to Delhi in about ten days' time. By plane, of course, and probably on to Chungking – just like that, as briskly and prosaically as though he were being asked to pop across the road and mail a letter. 'All right for you, I suppose?' said Arbuthnot, squinting up at him. Mark thought of Janet briefly before he nodded and said 'Fine', and they settled down to details. When he finally got back to his own office, he still couldn't believe it. After over four years of sitting in one place with his nose to the grindstone, the idea of getting on a plane and going somewhere made him feel like a child let out of school. The whole job might take six months, Arbuthnot had said. The only unpleasant part ahead was telling Janet, but he'd get over that somehow. She would have to go down to his mother's – hard on the old lady, who would have Janet, Bill, and Sally added to the ever-ravenous land girls, but it would be a bit of company for them all while he was away. Anyway, other men's wives were having to face infinitely worse separations every day, and it was probably about time that Janet had her share.

When he opened his front door that evening, his house greeted him with the chilly air of a home unswept, unwarmed, ungarnished. A jumble of garments and muddy gum boots in the hall indicated that the charitable neighbour had brought the children home and, judging by sounds from above, was now trying to get them to bed. Mark went up to the nursery and said, 'Mrs. Stevens, you ought to have a medal struck for this. Don't you stay a minute longer. I'll finish them off.' The charitable neighbour, looking relieved, said, 'Well, I *have* got Mr. Stevens' supper to get, but I'll be over in the morning first thing to see how Mrs. Goring is,' and went off. Mark took off his coat, set Bill to shovelling cereal and milk into his sister's mouth and went along to Janet.

She looked flushed and harassed, lying huddled up in a little pink knitted jacket.

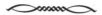

'I'll be up tomorrow,' she said. 'The house must be looking awful.'

'You'll stay right there,' said Mark. 'Mrs. Stevens and I are doing fine. We hardly miss you at all.' I won't tell her about Delhi tonight, he thought. I'll wait until she's feeling a bit better, poor thing.

'Mark, Bill ought to have some Syrup of Figs,' Janet said. 'I'm sure Mrs. Stevens hasn't given him any.'

'All right,' he said, 'I'll see to it.'

He shook up the pillows, collected some dirty things, and went out. 'I don't suppose the hens have been shut up,' she called hoarsely after him. Mark could almost feel affectionate towards the hens tonight. But what, he wondered, did one do with nine Rhode Island Reds when one unexpectedly went to India? Perhaps the invaluable Mrs. Stevens could come to the rescue there too. Going back to the nursery, he transferred all the cereal that wasn't on the floor into Bill's mouth, sat Sally expertly on her pot, and finally got them both pinned down in their cots. Then he went downstairs and started to wash up the debris. What did you do in the Great War of Decision, Daddy? Stood at the sink, my boy, and got the sticky cereal unglued from your spoon. But only ten more nights and he'd be on his way. The hot-water boiler stood looking at him like a cold, malevolent black goblin, and he remembered that he must light it up. The kitchen looked in a fearful mess, too. It was some time before he had it straight and went up to Janet with a cup of Ovaltine and a fresh hot-water bottle.

'Poor Mark!' she said. 'I do hate to see you do this.'

'Don't you worry,' he said. 'I love it.'

He sat down on her bed with his arm round her shoulders while she drank the Ovaltine.

'By the way,' he said, 'do you remember Nigel Travers? We met him and his wife – big, fair girl – dancing at the Berkeley one night, remember? Well, he's been killed with the parachute chaps.' He couldn't stop the note of irritation from creeping into his voice. 'Last man in the world you'd have expected to join an outfit like that, somehow. He was older than me, you know.'

'Dancing at the Berkeley,' Janet said slowly. 'It seems an awful time ago.' To his surprise, she suddenly began to cry. 'I suppose you wish it were you,' she sobbed. 'You wish you'd gone off with Nigel Travers and jumped out of planes and got killed.'

'Darling, don't be an idiot,' said Mark.

'Yes, you do, you do,' she said, crying bitterly.

Eventually he got her calmed down and went downstairs again to lay the breakfast table for the morning, put the milk bottles out, and, as an afterthought, try to find himself a snack in the larder. He collected some bread and cheese and a bottle of beer and carried them into the living-room. The nine o'clock news was just coming on. An order of the day from Marshal Stalin, said the calm B.B.C. voice . . . and heavy fighting is in progress . . . and the Admiralty regrets to announce. . . . Somewhere or other, thought Mark, munching his bread and cheese, it's still going on. For men crouching in a muddy ditch, struggling in oily water, it had at least the bitter satisfaction of something seen in the round, not simply a column of figures locked in a government briefcase. Ten

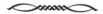

days from now, he thought, feeling suddenly lighter-hearted. As he stood at the sink later on, washing up the last, positively the last bloody plate of the day, he heard the bombers from the nearby flying field beginning to go over on the night's assignment. They droned slowly, purposefully, as regularly as buses passing down Piccadilly, over the house, the children sleeping in their cots, Janet feverishly dozing in the untidy bedroom which must worry her so much, poor dear.

Pretty soon he went up to bed. Janet moved restlessly as he switched off the light and lay down. I'll wait for two or three days more, thought Mark, and then I'll have to tell her. As he lay staring in front of him, listening to the still steady roar of the bombers, he pictured himself sitting in the plane, working at a bunch of papers on his knees, and suddenly a little speck appearing in the distance. The man sitting behind him leaned forward sharply. 'Messerschmitt,' he said curtly. It could happen, thought Mark, it could happen perfectly well. And he lay smiling, listening to Janet cough, and hugging the thought that danger was as possible for him after all as it was for Nigel Travers or the next man.

THE DANGER

8 July 1944

⟨⚬⚬⚬⚬⚬⟩

Mrs. Dudley's evacuees had gone at last, and an almost supernatural hush had seemed to descend upon the house and garden the moment they left. As joyfully as cats plunging back into a dustbin, they had returned to London, without expressing gratitude or regret, without giving a shadow of a sign that four years of living in the midst of what Mrs. Dudley called Beauty had made the slightest impression on them. The Rudds had remained sturdily impervious to Beauty right up to the last. On a morning when Mrs. Dudley's magnolias were bursting wide in the sunshine and patches of frosty Alpine blues and yellows were beginning to dapple the rockery, where Mr. Dudley's terrible old gardening hat could be seen slowly moving, Mrs. Rudd had stood gazing out of the window with an eye only too clearly nostalgic for a good Woolworth's. 'Ever so quiet, isn't it?' she had said, staring contemptuously at a gentian. 'Might be miles and miles from everything, really, instead of only ten minutes' walk from the village.' 'That's what we like about the house,' Mrs. Dudley had replied, to which Mrs. Rudd had said forgivingly, 'Well, everyone to his taste, of course,' and flung the lipsticked stub of her cigarette out into Beauty's face before getting on with her lackadaisical pushing of a mop over the hall parquet.

It had been part of the agreement, when the Rudds arrived, that Mrs. Rudd, besides keeping their own quarters clean, should assist about the house. Both these clauses, Mrs. Dudley had speedily discovered, were mere light-hearted figures of speech, for Mrs. Rudd was a slut. The word seemed to have been invented for her. Now that the Rudds had gone, now that the beautiful, incredible silence had settled down over a house empty of strangers again, the full horror of Mrs. Rudd could be relished, like the details of an appalling illness mercifully past: the mane of yellow hair which became brunette an inch from the parting, the broad bottom in navy-blue slacks. Mrs. Rudd had donned trousers at the beginning of the war and was perpetually ready to hoist the yardarm or do any other athletic exercises which might be required of her. For shopping in the village, Mrs. Dudley, who was conservative, had considered that the costume was excessive, but Mrs. Rudd had clung to the navy-blue pants, to which she had added a revealing sweater on chilly days and a flimsy blouse, unbuttoned to interesting limits, on hot ones. In winter, to prove that she was a cut above the ordinary evacuee caste, Mrs. Rudd had also donned a short jacket, made out of the fur of some depressed, yellowish animal that, like Mrs. Rudd's hair, seemed somewhat undecided at the partings. Mr. Dudley, leaving his garden long enough to potter down to the village and collect his monthly bottle of Scotch, always shrank back nervously into the shop if he spotted the Rudd cavalcade coming up the street – Sonny in

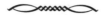

the push chair, Marlene and Marina trotting either side of the jaunty maternal behind. It was curious, he reported mildly to Mrs. Dudley, what a really libidinous effect high heels had when combined with tight trousers, a fur monkey jacket, and shoulder-length golden hair. He had mentioned a few Biblical characters of whom he had been irresistibly reminded as he watched their evacuee languidly shopping for Marina's corn flakes and Sonny's Syrup of Figs.

Mrs. Rudd had also departed from the usual evacuee pattern by having a husband with her, a silent, seemingly melancholy man who was employed by a firm which had moved its files and office staff out of bombing reach. To Messrs. Brown, Clutterbuck & Brown's sudden stout conviction that the worst of the blitzes was over, Mrs. Dudley now owed the unspeakable beatitude of being rid of the Rudds. She could hardly believe that she would never again have to listen to the marital difficulties, the embarrassing confidences, which had oozed from Mrs. Rudd as she slapped a duster over the drawing-room china of a morning. Sometimes Mrs. Dudley had felt her colour deepening guiltily when she encountered Mr. Rudd and his pipe mooning round the garden in the evenings. 'Still waters run deep,' Mrs. Rudd had often significantly observed, with a side swipe of the duster at some particularly frail Chelsea nymph. 'There's no knowing with those quiet types, is there? I suppose I didn't ought to have married Harold, really. When I had my figure, there were no heights I couldn't have attempted, the variety stage included.' 'Well, you've got your children as compensation,' Mrs. Dudley would suggest soothingly. And Mrs. Rudd would admit that there were always the kiddies – or the kidlets, as she some-times, in moments of acute maternal affection, called them. Marlene and Marina seemed to be trying to make up for her disappointment over the variety stage by eternally practising the dancing, their soiled hair ribbons waggling up and down, their small, sharp faces solemn as they hoofed in almost perfect unison on the gravel or along the passage, when Mr. Dudley was taking an afternoon nap. Sonny, a pasty-faced child, lived on a diet of his own and his parents' sweet ration, alternated with copious draughts of Syrup of Figs. Mrs. Rudd dealt out sticky kisses and smart cuffs impartially to her brood, but when Mrs. Dudley's married sons, John and Andrew, came down on leave, her tigerish fondness for the kidlets seemed to wane. On these occasions the rolling blue eye and the voluptuous curves appeared to roll and curl even more suggestively, her blouses get more flimsy, their buttons still more precarious. 'My God, that woman!' Andrew had groaned, raiding Mr. Dudley's Scotch after a sudden ambush in the rose garden. 'She's a shocker. You'll have to get rid of her, Mother. Ring up Miss Sykes and say they'll have to find her another billet.'

'I've rung up Nancy Sykes until I'm tired of it,' Mrs. Dudley said despairingly. 'She always says that this is the only house that can take them all, and she prefers not to split up families. Sometimes I think they're here forever.'

The taxi had come for them, finally. Sonny's push chair had been strapped on top. Mr. Rudd had seemed to be on the verge of struggling to say something fitting before he gave it up

and turned to help with the luggage. For the journey, Mrs. Rudd's plump calves had emerged from the stern sexlessness of women at war and were sleek in tan rayon below the hem of her check costume. 'I daresay the place will seem ever so funny without us,' she exclaimed to Mrs. Dudley, pushing the head of Marina's kitten back into its basket. Sure enough, after the taxi had disappeared down the drive, with Mr. Rudd waving radiantly like a bride from among the armfuls of flowers which Marina and Marlene had selected from the borders, the place did seem funny. In the silence of the house starting immediately to settle back comfortably into character again, Mrs. Dudley reflected that its inmates could also settle back into character – an elderly couple of quiet interests, getting on with their small, puttering war jobs and their gardening. The brassy nightmare interlude of the Rudds was over.

The house, she thought, seemed not only funny but positively eerie. She stood in the hall, listening for the gramophone, Mrs. Rudd's cigarette cough, Sonny whining, Marina and Marlene going shuffle, shuffle, stomp, stomp along the kitchen passage, Mrs. Rudd humming 'Yours' in a fruity contralto as she slopped tea leaves into the sink. Silence, nothing but rich, soaking silence. True, their smell remained in the rooms they had occupied – a stale, close smell, in which it was possible to identify face powder, food, Sonny's white mice, Mr. Rudd's pipe, and Mrs. Rudd. Mrs. Dudley, violently flinging open windows, wondered whether she should burn a fumigating candle, as though the Rudds had been an infectious disease.

But happiness was beginning to steal over her. She gave up

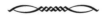

trying to do anything, and went out into the hall and started drifting aimlessly from room to room, luxuriously listening to their emptiness. She couldn't remember when she had last felt so happy.

There was nothing to warn Mrs. Dudley that this halcyon peace was threatened when, one morning a week or so after the Rudds had left, the front doorbell rang. It was a perfect morning, Mrs. Dudley had just noted contentedly, and the garden was beginning to look its very best. She still could not quite believe that at any moment the kidlets would not come whooping from the rockery, their fists full of her most precious Alpines, or that Mrs. Rudd would not be issuing forth, cigarette dangling from her lips, to shake out a duster and gaze round hungrily for the postman or any stray titbit in trousers to sweeten the howling wilderness. But thank God it was true, thought Mrs. Dudley cheerfully, on her way through her clean, silent house to open the front door.

The girl standing on the doorstep, a thin young woman without a hat, said, 'Mrs. Dudley? My name is Rachel Craig, and I'm a friend of your daughter-in-law's. Peg said that you wouldn't mind my coming along to see you.'

'Do come in, won't you?' said Mrs. Dudley. 'And forgive my looking so untidy. Peg may have told you that, like most people these days, we've got no servants at all. Are you staying somewhere down here?'

'No,' the girl said. 'That's just the point. I'm not staying down here, but I want to be. Peg thought that you might be able to help.'

An appalling suspicion entered Mrs. Dudley's head, but it was too late to do anything – to say that she was the char woman, for instance, and that Mrs. Dudley was out. They sat down in the living-room, round which the visitor gazed appreciatively. 'How lovely to see a real home again, after all the furnished lodgings I've been in,' she said. 'I suppose some time George and I will have a home of our own.' She smiled at Mrs. Dudley, who smiled warily back. 'He's been stationed down here, at the camp over at Fairfield,' the girl said. 'Of course he doesn't know for how long I've been trying to get rooms somewhere near for me and Evelyn – that's my baby – but everywhere is so full up with evacuees and things, isn't it? Anyway, I was nearly despairing, and then I ran into Peg in London yesterday, and she said perhaps you'd be willing to take us as paying guests.'

For a wild moment, Mrs. Dudley thought of saying, 'Look here, I'm alone and in peace for the first time in four years. I'm sick to death of strangers in my house. Won't you please go away?' But the impulse to be brutally candid passed, and the baser instinct to slide out of it somehow, with as much social grace as possible, overcame Mrs. Dudley. She heard her own voice saying instantly, plausibly, 'I'm sorry. I'd like to help you out, but I simply haven't the room.'

Mrs. Craig's glance wandered gently round the big living-room and out into the spacious airiness of the hall. 'Evelyn and I would tuck up in any corner,' she said. 'You wouldn't know we were here, really. She's a very good baby.'

But even good babies yell sometimes, Mrs. Dudley thought. They yell, their napkins simmer perpetually on the stove and festoon the bathroom, they start to crawl and then to toddle like homing pigeons straight for the rockery and the Alpines. The Craigs, coming for weeks, might stay for years, as the Rudds had done. Sonny Rudd had arrived a pasty infant in arms; he had left still pasty but hideously active, capable of all forms of small-boy mischief. And how do I know, thought Mrs. Dudley in a panic, that your George won't turn out to be another quiet type like Mrs. Rudd's Harold, and you'll tell me about it day in, day out, pinned up against my own kitchen wall, where I can't escape? She began to explain that there really wasn't all that space, because she had to keep rooms ready for her sons and their wives when they came on leave. Then there were the grandchildren, who spent their school holidays with her. John's boy and girl, as she spoke of them, mysteriously multiplied and became troops of boys and girls, pouring home every few weeks with their hockey sticks and cricket bats.

Mrs. Craig, interrupting as though she hadn't really been following, said, 'I'd be awfully glad to help with the house. I'm a good cook – or George used to think so. You see, if only we could be somewhere not too far away, so that he could see us sometimes, before he gets sent goodness knows where, it will make all the difference.'

With terror in her heart, Mrs. Dudley felt that the Craigs were taking shape, were becoming as threateningly real and three-dimensional as the Rudds. In another moment, the noises of a fresh set of alien lives would be invading the privacy of her quiet house. She would have to get used all over again to alien sounds – to Mrs. Craig's way of coughing, of running upstairs, to George's motor bike on the drive, to their bath water running, their voices murmuring. In another moment she would give in. Feeling hypocritical, hating herself, she said smoothly, 'I do feel so sorry for all you young people and I wish I could have managed it. But there it is. It's really too bad of Peg to send you down on a wild-goose chase like this.'

Mrs. Craig's disappointed face looked suddenly very young and sharp round the cheekbones. The furnished lodgings, thought Mrs. Dudley with a pang, possibly didn't do very well in the way of food.

After that, the visit crumpled. On their way to the door, Mrs. Dudley suggested a name or two – had she tried there? Yes, Mrs. Craig had. Everywhere was full, Mrs. Craig said, trying to smile and not succeeding, in a perfectly adult way. She shook hands and walked away down the drive, and Mrs. Dudley went briskly back into the house like a woman expecting at any moment a sudden influx of grandchildren. In the living-room she sat down limply, with a feeling of weakness round the knees and drew a long, quivering breath of relief. The danger was over and she felt shamefacedly pleased with herself, as though she had been clever in a way which didn't bear examining too closely. She began telling herself quickly that it was really too much to ask, coming too soon after four nightmare years of being pressed to the suffocating, slatternly bosom of Mrs. Rudd. I'm not so young as I was, she told herself. I've done my bit and more. Everyone says so.

Presently she glanced at the clock and calculated that Mrs. Craig must be nearly at the station. She wouldn't feel

entirely safe until after the London train had gone, though. The familiar light stutter of the little French clock was soothing. The clock, a branch of roses tapping against the window, the claws of the old terrier clicking across the hall parquet – there was not a sound in her own quiet house which she could not identify. We are alone together, they said. We belong to you and to nobody else. She waited for the usual rush of pure happiness to flood over her at the thought, as it had done so many times since the Rudds' taxi bore them away. But today something was wrong, for nothing happened. Nothing at all thought Mrs. Dudley, staring miserably at the clock, which soon told her that the London train would now be steaming out of the station.

THE WASTE OF IT ALL

16 December 1944

Philip had been in the Middle East for over three years now, and sometimes it seemed to Frances even longer than that. They had been married very soon after meeting each other and he had been sent abroad a few months later. Sometimes, in a panic, Frances would close her eyes and try to remember Philip's face in detail, how he smiled, how his voice sounded. On good days he came to life perfectly, but if she was tired or depressed she could bring him back only in fragments that wouldn't connect, like a jigsaw puzzle from which the key pieces were lost. Or if eventually she assembled him, he wouldn't work in her head. He'd stand looking at her dumbly, not smiling, and she would have the disconcerting feeling that he was some stranger she had met and liked at a party but couldn't give more than a name and a face to.

Of course letters helped to keep them in touch. Philip wrote long, full letters by every mail, and so did Frances. But sometimes she would be brought up short by the realisation that her chatter was stuffed with all the mental and physical debris acquired in the three years without him – allusions to friends he had never met, books he hadn't read, little jokes which they hadn't laughed at first together – and that Philip must, at times, try to fit together his own jigsaw Frances and fail miserably. Worst of all to her was the awful suspicion that she had almost grown used to doing without him. For the first two years she had missed him unbearably, but now her loneliness was something which she put on automatically when she got up and hardly noticed any more, like a person who had become accustomed to wearing glasses or a false limb.

Frances wrote a lot about the cottage, for she knew that Philip enjoyed the smallest, silliest details. He had wanted, touchingly, to leave her in their own home. He had an old-fashioned wish to frame a woman in a setting which would include a fire, a lamp, and a work box, and he had hated Frances's undomestic plan of getting into the uniform of the first service that would have her. They had found the cottage on one of his last leaves, a Hans Andersen place into which someone with taste had fitted less elfin modern plumbing and other conveniences. 'On a good train service to London, too,' Philip had pointed out. 'It's really a buy. If we ever want to sell we'll be able to get twice what we're giving, before the war's over.' But she knew that he didn't want her to sell. He liked thinking of her there, safely anchored, something to come home to. He had always been fond of drawing little plans of things, and his letters were full of diagrams explaining to Frances what she was to have done about a leaking bit of the thatch roof, where the hen house was to go, exactly how he wanted the new apple trees planted. He was a countryman by birth,

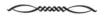

a Londoner only by adoption, and he loved that sort of thing.

Frances, a Londoner by birth and a countrywoman by adoption, grappled valiantly with thatch, hens, and orchard in the intervals of a full-time job at a government office which had been evacuated to the neighbourhood. A series of women friends and their children had shared the cottage with her. She became used to the light clip of feminine conversation, to light eating on trays. When a man came to the house, his voice seemed to roar like a giant's and the floors seemed to shudder under his unaccustomed tread.

One day the supply of women friends ran out, and Frances, wildly bicycling round, couldn't find a soul who was free to come and clean the place and have a meal waiting for her when she got home in the evenings. She was on the point of giving up, Philip or no Philip, and retreating thankfully to London, where thatch didn't leak and eggs were to be had conveniently dried from grocery store shelves, when Margaret suddenly happened.

'I'm delighted about Margaret,' Philip wrote some weeks later. 'Now, perhaps, you'll get some decent food to eat. So far as I can make out, you and the girl friends have been getting along on lettuce and cups of tea. Your description of the Home where you found her chilled my blood. Pure Dickens, my God! She must think it's heaven now she and the kid are with you, darling.'

Frances, folding Philip's letter, could hear Margaret singing in the kitchen above the sizzle of frying bacon and certainly sounding cheerful. Frances began to drink her coffee, thinking of the Home of the Good Samaritan, to which a friend's suggestion had sent her. Chilling, she thought, had been the word for it. Sitting uneasily on a hard sofa in the matron's parlour, a small room smelling frigidly of beeswax and charity, she had looked out into the sunshine where four or five unmarried mothers were pushing prams up and down the gravel walks.

'We have to be very careful, of course, where we place our girls,' the matron was saying. 'Once they make a mistake of this kind, they so often get into – well, the habit, you might say.' She looked at Frances piercingly, as though suspecting her of keeping a bordello. 'You say you're at work all day. Would Margaret be likely to see any men while you're out?'

Frances thought swiftly of the lad who delivered the papers, a grubby urchin of twelve, and of old Bostock, the gardener, who hobbled in two afternoons a week to dig the vegetables. She felt justified in answering, 'None, absolutely none,' and the matron, after thoughtful survey of Frances's wedding ring, agreed that Margaret and the baby should go to her next day.

'The father won't worry you – that's one thing,' the matron said. 'One of these soldiers – married, of course. Somewhere on the Continent now, I suppose, and never a thought for the poor girls, you may be sure.' She sniffed and her uniform crackled indignantly.

'It's a lovely baby anyway,' said Frances. 'They always are,' said the matron, sniffing again, as though she would have preferred the wages of sin to be a little less blatantly plump, dimpled, and thriving.

Frances wrote back to Philip and told him that it was a great success. Margaret was a good cook and, in her satisfaction at being delivered out of the Samaritan bosom, she cleaned the place with a ferocity which echoed in Frances's ears as she bicycled off in the mornings. Margaret was a big, fat girl with a remarkably plain face; Frances could only suppose that the acute homesickness of one of the visiting warriors had been responsible for Margaret's baby, Raymond. None of the friends who had shared the cottage had had very young children, and it was extraordinary what a difference Raymond made in the household. Frances had always felt that the cottage had the shallow, rootless air of a temporary wartime home, but now it began to look as though the people living there didn't intend to move away. Washing billowed permanently from Margaret's line between the two old pear trees. Frances had managed to borrow a pram and a cot, which old Bostock had fixed up, and Raymond slept or philosophically examined the sky all day out on the little patch of lawn.

At the beginning, thinking of Bostock, of the milk girl, whose nose was an inquisitive red button as she clumped past the pram with the bottles, Frances had said to Margaret, 'Would it be easier if we called you Mrs. Judd? It might sort of settle things, mightn't it?'

'I wouldn't feel natural as a missis,' Margaret said comfortably. 'Miss Judd I am and Miss Judd I'll probably stop, and Raymond will have to take it as he finds it. There'll be plenty like him, I daresay.'

Frances had carried the baby out of the kitchen and was playing with him on the living-room sofa. 'Why did you call him Raymond?' she asked. 'Was it his father's name?'

'No, it wasn't,' said Margaret. 'His father's name was George – or he said it was, anyway.' She laughed. 'But I always thought if I got married and had a little boy, I'd call him Raymond. Well, the war happened and I didn't get married, but I got Raymond.'

'It's a beautiful name,' Frances said warmly.

She bought some wool and began knitting for the baby in the evenings. He had very few clothes or other possessions, and when she went to London for a couple of days' leave, she found that he kept coming into her thoughts, and she bought a little hairbrush with a pale-blue back, a rattle, and a blue sleeping bag. 'If your baby is an active little fellow, this will keep him snug in all weathers,' the saleswoman had said as she folded up the sleeping bag, and Frances, somehow enjoying the atmosphere of this shop, where every customer was automatically a mother, said seriously, 'Well, yes, he *is* the active type of baby.' She felt matronly and amused with herself, and wondered if the saleswoman's eyeglasses would focus less starrily if she knew that the sleeping bag was intended to wrap a nameless Baby Bunting, whose daddy had gone a-hunting and wasn't likely to come back. 'Won't he love the ducky pink rabbit on it!' snuffled the saleswoman with a damp blend of sentiment and catarrh. Here mother-hood was strictly the legitimate article. Frances, conscientiously building up detail, stopped and fingered some tiny night-dresses, assuming the correct brooding expression, on her way to the door. Once outside, she relaxed and began thinking what a funny description she would make out of her shopping in her next letter to Philip. But somehow, though she had been entertained while it was happening, it no longer seemed particularly amusing when she got home, and she put the idea out of her head rather abruptly.

Her homecoming was really very pleasant. There was a letter from Philip waiting for her, and Margaret had got splendid fires going and something good cooking for supper. About a month before, Frances had bought a puppy, because everyone said that a dog was such good company. He was a spaniel puppy, christened Bruce, and now, in a frenzy of welcome, he rushed round the room, fell on her shoes, and sprinkled her affectionately with water. Raymond was also brought in to see her, and though she had been away only two days, she insisted that he had grown. He was really beautiful – not in the least like Margaret, she thought. The unknown George must have been good-looking. Raymond's small face was an obvious duplicate of someone's strong family face which for generations had been transmitting bright-blue eyes, fresh colour, and a straight nose. Frances thought what a sensation he would have caused if she had been able to take him along and show him off to that woman who had burbled about the ducky pink rabbit.

She produced the sleeping bag and other things and Margaret flushed with pleasure. 'It's beautiful!' she said again and again.

'Well, we shan't have to worry now about keeping him warm in the garden,' Frances said lightly.

She sat down to read Philip's letter, with Bruce cuddled beside her. The little fret of someone besides herself in the room was oddly companionable. There was no doubt, she thought, a dog did make a difference, and spaniels were always so devoted. She stroked his curly ears absently as she read. Philip wrote gloomily, for he had thought that he was getting leave and it had fallen through. He had taken bets that the war would be over by Christmas, but now he was feeling less certain. 'What I mind most is the waste of it all,' he wrote. 'Waste of time, waste of you, waste of the good things we could be doing together.' Later on he made an obvious effort to sound more cheerful, and went into details of some plan for the garden, illustrated with one of his usual neat little maps. Although the time he had spent at the cottage could be counted in days, every inch of its terrain, every twig, every stone seemed to be printed photographically on his memory. It's really the only link we've had, Frances thought. The only place we've known together, the sticks and stones we share.

Frances put down Philip's letter and sat looking into the fire. She could hear Margaret and Raymond in the kitchen. He had his bath in the evening and usually she enjoyed watching, but this evening she didn't feel in the mood. Margaret had put down the sleeping bag and other odds and ends when she drew the curtains and she had forgotten to take them to the kitchen with her. Frances picked up the hairbrush and began turning it over in her hands. It had flowers hand-painted on its blue back, and it struck her that perhaps it had been idiotic to choose such frivolities for one whose path would possibly not be particularly flowery. Margaret might take him away at any time and, if she did, Frances hated to think what might happen to them. Maybe it was silly to spoil him like this, as though life could guarantee to wrap him permanently in softest blue wool, guarded by ducky pink rabbits, amused by a bauble of little bells tied up with corals. Frances could hear the splashing of water in the kitchen and a gurgle of enjoyment from Raymond, then Margaret's voice murmuring something. Unexpectedly Frances felt a pang of irritation against Margaret for having been so stupid or so wanton that Raymond must always be bathed in front of some stranger's fire. Now that she came to think of it, the girl's jolly, phlegmatic acceptance of her lot was also irritating. That business about being called Mrs. Judd, for instance. If she had thought at all of Raymond's future, she would have fallen in with that suggestion. Frances could have bought her a wedding ring, and they could have agreed on some tale of widowhood which would sound plausible in a village full of women whose men had died as far from home, as quietly, as Frances would have arranged for George to die. She couldn't help feeling indignant when she thought how casual Margaret had been about everything. She's really nothing but a stupid peasant, Frances thought angrily.

Somehow, somewhere, the pleasantness of getting home had escaped. Frances picked up Philip's letter to read it again, and then, for the first time, she noticed that Bruce had got down from the sofa. The little dog was standing beside the

door that led into the kitchen; he was snuffling deeply under the crack and every now and then he scratched hopefully. He liked Margaret, who had a way with animals. Once or twice lately, Frances had searched for him and found him curled up on the kitchen chair, and, though she had laughed, she had always carried him out firmly and closed the door tightly behind her. Now he was scratching and whining to get in. Frances called to him sharply. He took no notice and a wave of quite ridiculous anger seized her. She got up, took the puppy by the scruff of his neck so roughly that he squeaked protestingly, and dumped him back on the sofa. 'You stay where you are!' she told him, and as she hit him across his blunt baby nose, she could hardly see him for the tears in her eyes and the dreadful empty feeling in her heart.

Letter from London

11 June 1944

For the English, D Day might well have stood for Dunkirk Day. The tremendous news that British soldiers were back on French soil seemed suddenly to reveal exactly how much it had rankled when they were beaten off it four years ago. As the great fleets of planes roared toward the coast all day long, people glancing up at them said, 'Now they'll know how our boys felt on the beaches at Dunkirk.' And as the people went soberly back to their jobs, they had a satisfied look, as though this return trip to France had in itself been worth waiting four impatient, interminable years for. There was also a slightly bemused expression on most D Day faces, because the event wasn't working out quite the way anybody had expected. Londoners seemed to imagine that there would be some immediate, miraculous change, that the heavens would open, that something like the last trumpet would sound. What they definitely hadn't expected was that the greatest day of our times would be just the same old London day, with men and women going to the office, queuing up for fish, getting haircuts, and scrambling for lunch.

D Day sneaked up on people so quietly that half the crowds flocking to business on Tuesday morning didn't know it was anything but Tuesday, and then it fooled them by going right on being Tuesday. The principal impression one got on the streets was that nobody was smiling. The un-English urge to talk to strangers which came over Londoners during the blitzes, and in other recent times of crisis, was noticeably absent. Everybody seemed to be existing wholly in a preoccupied silence of his own, a silence which had something almost frantic about it, as if the effort of punching bus tickets, or shopping for kitchen pans, or whatever the day's chore might be, was, in its quiet way, harder to bear than a bombardment. Later in the day, the people who patiently waited in the queues at each news-stand for the vans to turn up with the latest editions were still enclosed in their individual silences. In the queer hush, one could sense the strain of a city trying to project itself across the intervening English orchards and cornfields, across the strip of water, to the men already beginning to die in the French orchards and cornfields which once more had become 'over there'. Flag sellers for a Red Cross drive were on the streets, and many people looked thoughtfully at the little red paper symbol before pinning it to their lapels, for it was yet another reminder of the personal loss which D Day was bringing closer for thousands of them.

In Westminster Abbey, typists in summer dresses and the usual elderly visitors in country-looking clothes came in to pray beside the tomb of the last war's Unknown Soldier, or to gaze rather vacantly at the tattered colours and the marble heroes of battles which no longer seemed remote. The top-hatted old warrior who is gatekeeper at Marlborough House, where King George V was born, pinned on all his medals in honour of the day, and hawkers selling cornflowers and red and white peonies had hastily concocted little patriotic floral arrangements, but there was no rush to put out flags, no cheers, no outward emotion. In the shops, since people aren't specially interested in spending money when they are anxious, business was extremely bad. Streets which normally are crowded had the deserted look of a small provincial town on a wet Sunday afternoon. Taxi drivers, incredulously cruising about for customers, said that it was their worst day in months. Even after the King's broadcast was over, Londoners stayed home. Everybody seemed to feel that this was one night you wanted your own thoughts in your own chair. Theatre and cinema receipts slumped, despite the movie houses' attempt to attract audiences by broadcasting the King's speech and the invasion bulletins. Even the pubs didn't draw the usual cronies. At midnight, London was utterly quiet, the Civil Defence people were standing by for a half-expected alert which didn't come, and D Day had passed into history.

It is in the country districts just away from the sealed south coast that one gets a real and urgent sense of what is happening only a few minutes' flying time away. Pheasants whirr their alarm at the distant rumble of guns, just as they did when Dunkirk's guns were booming. On Tuesday evening, villagers hoeing weeds in the wheat fields watched the gliders passing in an almost unending string towards Normandy. And always there are the planes. When the big American bombers sail overhead, moving with a sinister drowsiness in their perfect formations, people who have not bothered to glance up at the familiar drone for months rush out of their houses to stare. Everything is different, now that the second front has opened, and every truck on the road, every piece of gear on the railways, every jeep and half-track which is heading toward the front has become a thing of passionate concern. The dry weather, which country folk a week ago were hoping would end, has now become a matter for worry the other way round. Farmers who wanted grey skies for their hay's sake now want blue ones for the sake of their sons, fighting in the skies and on the earth across the Channel. Finally, there are the trainloads of wounded, which are already beginning to pass through summer England, festooned with its dog roses and honeysuckle. The red symbol which Londoners were pinning to their lapels on Tuesday now shines on the side of trains going past crossings where the waiting women, shopping baskets on their arms, don't know whether to wave or cheer or cry. Sometimes they do all three.

AFTERWORD

Mollie Panter-Downes and *The New Yorker*

⌒⌒⌒⌒⌒

The writer of Mollie Panter-Downes's obituary in *The Guardian* divined that she was 'one of those writers who will, without doubt, be rediscovered.'[1] She left a legacy of fiction- and fact-writing remarkable for its breadth, depth and – curiously – its neglect. Thirty-six short stories have remained dormant since their first appearance in *The New Yorker*. Twenty-one of these have been collected for the first time in this book.* There will certainly be subsequent collections of her *New Yorker* fiction. The recent unearthing of a short story in the July 1935 issue of *Argosy* promises future discoveries of her uncollected work.

There is the importance of rediscovery here. But there is also the question of why Mollie Panter-Downes never sought to preserve her contribution to the short-story genre, despite her obvious commitment to it. Moreover, where do the stories fit into her corpus? And what were the reciprocating influences during her relationship with *The New Yorker*? The statistics speak for themselves. Over an extraordinary fifty years, from 1938 to 1987, she published 852 pieces in the

*Only 'Goodbye, My Love' and 'In Clover' have previously been reprinted.

magazine. The range of her contributions is as impressive as the sum. It includes poems, short stories, London Letters, book reviews, Profiles, Letters from England, Far Flung Correspondent pieces, Reporter at Large coverage, Onward and Upward with the Arts columns, and numerous one-off articles. The significance of her impact on this influential magazine becomes evident with the recognition that her total contribution far exceeds that of any British – and most American – writers.

Indeed, because of the sheer amount of her work in journalism and fiction – and the authority and reach of *The New Yorker*, in which the large majority of it appeared – hers is among the most versatile and perceptive voices in British women's writing of this period. It is a telling endorsement that her friend and contemporary Rebecca West, who also worked brilliantly but more famously in fiction and non-fiction, marvelled at her energy and style. In a letter congratulating her on a *New Yorker* piece, West said that her writing was 'of course perfection, you are a craftsman such as they don't make nowaday [sic], and your values are so good.'[2]

For most of her writing life, Mollie Panter-Downes was best-known for her journalism and considered herself, before anything else, a journalist. She averred, 'I'm a reporter. I can't invent.' Indeed, she held one of the most respected positions in weekly journalism, writing *The New Yorker's* Letter from London from 1939 to 1984. The 153 Letters written during the Second World War have attained the status coveted by every journalist. They have transcended their time and become an historical and human document of permanent

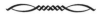

value, preserved in *Letters from England* (1940), and *London War Notes, 1939–1945* (1972). Eighteen of them appear in *The New Yorker Book of War Pieces* (1947 & 1989), along with the work of other lionised journalists of the decade, among them, A.J. Liebling, Rebecca West, John Hersey, Walter Bernstein, and Philip Hamburger.

If Mollie Panter-Downes's contribution to British journalism is so secure, why is she relatively unknown in her native land? What happened to her fiction? Her name may be unfamiliar in Britain because she was a *New Yorker* writer. At any time during her long tenure at the magazine, the British readership numbered between 1,000 and 6,000, while the American figures ranged from 400,000 to 800,000. Also, she held one of the magazine's cherished, but binding, 'First Reading Agreements', which required that it have the initial option on anything she wrote, fact or fiction, article or novel. She never wished to write for any other periodical or publisher. So, it is unsurprising and perhaps unfortunate that she became more famous in the United States than in her homeland. A description in a 1971 *Sunday Times* interview is apt: 'To the readers of *The New Yorker* magazine the name of Mollie Panter-Downes has spelled England since she became its London correspondent in 1939'. However, this relationship caused some confusion: 'she is so closely associated with the magazine that she is often thought . . . to be American'.[3]

Those to whom she was well known in Britain may have been relatively few, but among them were figures whose opinions spoke volumes. When collected as *London War Notes: 1939–1945*, her Letters from London were widely acclaimed in the press. Her papers contain numerous personal letters of praise from literary friends. Of the collection, Noël Coward wrote to say that 'it is so very well done and I am sodden with nostalgia.' John Betjeman joked, 'so good a writer as you must have another war.'[4]

She was in familiar company at *The New Yorker*. The magazine offered refuge to many British and Irish writers forced or lured to seek more money, prestige, and opportunity in American magazines at a time when the periodical market in Britain was in irreversible decline. A considerable number published the majority or nearly all of their total short-fiction output in *The New Yorker*. Among them are Sylvia Townsend Warner, Elizabeth Taylor, Frank O'Connor, Winifred Williams, V.S. Pritchett, Penelope Mortimer, and Penelope Gilliatt, to name but seven. Others published a significant, if smaller, amount, including Rebecca West, John Collier, Stephen Leacock, Edith Templeton, Roald Dahl, Rhys Davies, and Joyce Cary. Mollie Panter-Downes may have made more fiction contributions to *The New Yorker* than any other British or Irish writer except Warner, Gilliatt, and O'Connor, but she did not care to preserve them.

Without doubt, the large majority of writers who call themselves *New Yorker* writers end up publishing their *New Yorker* short stories in collections. It was not uncommon for them to publish collections consisting only of their *New Yorker* stories; Warner, Taylor, and Pritchett did it a number of times. Given the magazine's reputation for screening high-quality fiction, it is a *fait accompli* that the stories appearing in its pages will be of abiding interest to publishers. But Mollie

Panter-Downes decided that her thirty-six *New Yorker* short stories, published between 1938 and 1965, would appear only once. It seems extraordinary that a writer so committed to the form and so clearly endorsed by her editors did not collect her stories. She may have concluded that they were unworthy of book form. That she was draconian in her self-criticism is apparent. Of her five novels – *The Shoreless Sea* (1923), *The Chase* (1925), *Storm Bird* (1929), *My Husband Simon* (1931), and *One Fine Day* (1947) – she disowned all but the last, which was again recognised, upon its republication in 1985, as a marvellous, subtle evocation of post-war mood. (One can also see how it crystallises the situation and conditions sketched in variations throughout this collection.)

Perhaps Mollie Panter-Downes considered her fiction second to her journalism. If she sought to control her biography, she succeeded. Her obituaries linger on her Letters from London, mention *The Shoreless Sea* (because of her precocious age), briefly refer to *One Fine Day*, and dismiss her short stories entirely. She may have characterised herself as a journalist, but it was because of *The New Yorker*'s leap of faith and lasting commitment that she became one. It is not possible to discuss her career, in fact- or fiction-writing, without an understanding of what the magazine meant to her and she to it.

From the beginning, *The New Yorker*'s editors were charmed by her voice, subject matter, and point of view: she was so *English*. Her initial seven publications are fiction, the first of which is a poem entitled 'Spring with an English Poet', published on 30 April 1938. It is an ironic re-write of Robert Browning's 1842 'Home-Thoughts, From Abroad', playing off

his pining and nostalgia by envisioning the air full not of the sounds and smells of spring, but of Hitler's killing gas:

> Oh, to be in England
> Now that April's there,
> And whoever wakes in England
> Sees, some morning, unaware,
> That the elm-tree bole is blocked from view
> By a notice telling him what to do
> When vapours steal through the primrose wood
> And the gas-proof room turns out no good,
> While the chaffinch chokes on the orchard bough
> In England – now!

At that time, pieces like this perfectly suited the magazine's stance on serious subjects like the Depression and war: if they were to be handled at all, they must be handled with irony or humour.

Mollie Panter-Downes fitted in with the shaping force of Anglophilia in the magazine's early years. A subtle commitment to things British satisfied the identikit *New Yorker* readership, the 'cosmopolitan elite': born, living, or working in New York City or, at least, the Northeastern United States; upper-middle-class; white; urban; university educated; affluent; well travelled. The magazine's notion of its geographical boundaries implicitly embraced London and Paris as places that New Yorkers frequented and felt happy in. Founder and editor Harold Ross started the Paris Letter in 1925 and the London Letter in 1934 in order to get weekly reports on 'happenings' in the two capitals. The London/Paris focus had much to do with the magazine's and readership's cosmopolitan self-perception. The original purpose of the Letters was to keep readers in touch with the same subjects discussed in regular *New Yorker* departments – the books, plays, restaurants, movies, and exhibitions that literate, intelligent Londoners and Parisians were talking about. From 1934 to 1939, the London Letter gave the impression that the writer was a person of considerable means and leisure, visiting and reporting on art exhibitions, auctions, flower shows, political events and concerts with delicate taste.

When the gravity and newsworthiness of the Second World War convinced Ross to turn *The New Yorker* from a comic metropolitan weekly into a global magazine publishing serious journalism and fiction, Britain was an obvious subject. Ross's biographer notes that, during the Second World War, 'the Anglophile in him prayed for Britain'. He knew his Anglophile readership, too, and recognised their desire not only for *The New Yorker* to cover the war, but to support America's involvement in it: he 'suspected that some people wanted the United States to enter the war essentially to preserve the Empire'.[5]

Janet Flanner, the magazine's Paris correspondent, had also been writing the London Letter since 1934 when she got trapped by the war in California and was unable to return to Europe. Ross was in need of a new London-based writer. On the strength of her first factual piece, an article on Jewish refugee children submitted on spec, he selected Mollie Panter-Downes. When she took over the London Letter in July 1939, the magazine had yet to handle the war directly or seriously. Correspondence reveals that, during the early

months of her authorship, the editors wanted pieces that would suit the magazine's non-involvement and appeal to its brand of Anglophile. The first telegram inviting her to write as 'our London correspondent' asks: 'CAN YOU CABLE US UP TO 2,000 WORDS ON HUMAN RATHER THAN POLITICAL EVENTS LONDON & COUNTRY STOP'. Ensuing ones ask her to write about 'the motor show theatre' and a 'where-are-they-now piece telling what prominent Londoners [are] doing like Coward'.[6] Two months later, another editor wonders:

> Do you think there may be a paragraph or so some time on the subject of what is happening to school life in England? What of Oxford and Cambridge? Are they depleted or converted into camps or what? What has become of the youths who took what I believe was called the Oxford pledge, swearing that they would never enlist? What is happening on the playing fields of Eton?[7]

After weeks of her pleading, the editors allowed Mollie Panter-Downes to switch to dealing directly with the war, probably responding to Ross's recent decision to handle the subject seriously. She then offered a different kind of 'English' voice with which American readers could identify. Summing up the news and sentiments of the nation as a whole during war time, her Letters were devoured by American readers, received like reassuring notes from a relative at the front, which in a sense she was. In a manner at once elegant and down-to-earth, Panter-Downes transmitted the anxiety and fear, but also the underlying British resolve, and even . . . some of the black humor.[8]

During the same period, Rebecca West published more intimate pieces to serve as a kind of counterpoint to the London Letters. Because Mollie Panter-Downes wrote for an American audience and was unconstrained by the myriad and rapidly-obsolete details of the English daily press, her editor, William Shawn, claimed that her clear-sighted pieces served her native readers: 'our thousands of English subscribers are doubtless more interested in your Letters than in anything else we run.'[9] However, one English reader disagreed with Mollie Panter-Downes's post-war presentation of her country. Winifred Williams wrote to her editor, William Maxwell:

> And Bill – What a country! Don't read Mollie Panter-Downes any more – the poor dear lives in a different England from the rest of us. Taxation has us – the professional class and the proletariat – right down in the gutter, and life is so grey and harsh it's a wonder people don't just die from the weight of sadness on their hearts.[10]

Williams's observation is adroit. Mollie Panter-Downes did live in a different England, one that experienced and expressed life from an upper-middle-class perspective: stoicism, cheerfulness, and wit were her stock in trade. There was symbiosis between her writing and *The New Yorker*. Hers was the kind of English voice they wanted. Her *New Yorker* obituary captures it: 'She was, in short, thoroughly, bred-in-the-bone *English* . . . and it was this Englishness that gave her Letter from London such authority.'[11] Moreover, they did not want British life rendered 'grey and harsh'. The magazine was enchanted by both the idea and the embodiment of her. To them, she was 'a writer whose grace and restraint mirrored her personality.'[12] The veteran editor Brendan Gill confessed that, in her case,

> the appearance, the prose style, and even the name are indisputably one. Mollie is a classic English beauty – fair, blue-eyed, erect – and just such a person as should bear the hyphenated patronymic Panter-Downes . . . Her dispatches from bombed, burning, and, for all we knew at the time, dying England were unforgettable; to us and to our readers, she was as much an embodiment of the gallant English spirit as Churchill himself.[13]

To corroborate *The New Yorker*'s interest in this kind of persona and perspective, one need only read the work of other British regulars, like Warner and Taylor, to see the kinship. Indeed, Warner took refuge in the magazine when she believed her short stories to be 'too English for the English'.

Of equal relevance, Mollie Panter-Downes's mode of fiction was symbiotic with *The New Yorker*, not least because it closely resembled her fact-writing in voice, tone, and setting. Because of Ross's background in journalism and lack of experience with other kinds of writing, he demanded that editors subject short stories to the same standards as those applied to fact pieces. A result was 'journalistic fiction', in which writers were expected to observe journalistic

techniques in the creation of a short story: factual accuracy; complete information; straightforward narration; clear, concise language; unambiguous description of action; comprehensible ordering of events; full characterisation; no contrived conclusions. Editors required short stories to demonstrate at least four of the five W's – who, what, when, and where; the why and how were optional. A comment in a letter from William Shawn consolidates these predilections. Although referring to Mollie Panter-Downes's non-fiction, it is equally applicable to her fiction: 'the straight observation piece with personalities woven through . . . seems to be the type you're most sympathetic to; and certainly we like that type.'[14]

What is relevant to our understanding of Mollie Panter-Downes is not just what she wrote, but the environment in which she wrote. *The New Yorker* is legendary for the length of time it keeps its writers and the peerless devotion that they, in turn, bring to it. Mollie Panter-Downes was a paradigm. The magazine's archives retain the narrative of this relationship in hundreds of letters and cables written between her and her editors during nearly five decades of collaboration. The flow of mutual respect is uninterrupted. One letter in particular captures both the esteem and warmth in which *The New Yorker* held her. In late 1967, she wrote to William Shawn to hint at her suspicion that the magazine was tiring of her London Letter and was keeping her on out of a sense of duty. She suggests that she should relinquish her post. She could not have imagined Shawn's response, a pipe dream to any writer. It is worth reproducing at length:

What I have been thinking is that the magazine cherishes your London Letter, and that the magazine will accommodate itself to your own wishes. That is, if, clearly, you want to drop the letter altogether and devote yourself to long pieces, we will sadly, reluctantly accept your decision. If you would prefer to write the letter from time to time, however irregularly, that, too, would be acceptable to us. A fortnightly Letter is no longer necessary. You ask whether I am happy about the London Letter. I am utterly happy. No one else could do what you do. You seem to write a letter whenever a letter is called for, you don't miss anything momentous, you tell us precisely what we want to know, and you write with undiminished spirit and style and poetry and wit. Yes, you can make even disappointment readable. I don't like bad news, or no news, but if it comes to me in your words, I'm grateful . . . If you decide to give up London, I doubt whether we'd go on with it; I just don't know. Certainly, I have something less than enthusiasm for the idea of a London Letter written by somebody else. As far as I'm concerned, our Letter from London is by Mollie Panter-Downes.[15]

One cannot over-estimate how pivotal this kind of support is to a writer, and how it provides her with the confidence to continue writing. That is what Mollie Panter-Downes did. Although mostly recognised for her writing during the Second World War, her contributions extended well beyond that subject and decade. In a rare interview, she exulted that her life with *The New Yorker* had been 'one enthralling round' because Shawn gave her such elasticity of scope for her writing. She wrote in virtually every category of *New Yorker* journalism. Her spectrum of subjects is too wide to list without risking reader stupefaction.

Mollie Panter-Downes did what she chose, and, curiously, one of those choices was to stop writing short stories. The genre may have lost its appeal for her. She published only ten stories in the fifty-odd years between the end of the war and her death, her last in 1965. But she leaves an impressive body of work written during a critical, concentrated period of time.

Gregory LeStage

1   obituary in *The Guardian* op. cit.
2   Rebecca West to M P-D 11 May 1971, Mollie Panter-Downes Papers
3   Ernestine Carter op. cit.
4   Noel Coward to M P-D 26 August 1972, John Betjeman to M P-D c. 1972, M P-D Papers
5   Thomas Kunkel *Genius in Disguise: Harold Ross of The New Yorker* New York 1995 p. 348
6   St Clair McKelway to M P-D, 1 and 19 September 1939, *The New Yorker* Archives, New York Public Library
7   William Shawn to M P-D 11 November 1939, NYPL
8   Kunkel op. cit. p. 349
9   Shawn to M P-D 8 April 1941, NYPL
10 Winifred Williams to William Maxwell 8 October 1945, NYPL
11 Botsford op. cit.
12 Kunkel op. cit. p. 349
13 Brendan Gill *Here at The New Yorker* London 1975 pp. 339, 364
14 Shawn to M P-D 8 April 1941, NYPL
15 Shawn to M P-D 10 December 1967, NYPL

The Persephone Originals:

No. 1   *William – an Englishman* (1919) by Cicely Hamilton

No. 2   *Mariana* (1940) by Monica Dickens

No. 3   *Someone at a Distance* (1953) by Dorothy Whipple

No. 4   *Fidelity* (1915) by Susan Glaspell

No. 5   *An Interrupted Life: the Diaries and Letters of Etty Hillesum 1941–43*

No. 6   *The Victorian Chaise-longue* (1953) by Marghanita Laski

No. 7   *The Home-Maker* (1924) by Dorothy Canfield Fisher

No. 8   *Good Evening, Mrs. Craven: the Wartime Stories of Mollie Panter-Downes 1939–44*

No. 9   *Few Eggs and No Oranges: the Diaries of Vere Hodgson 1940–45*

No. 10   *Good Things in England* (1932) by Florence White

No. 11   *Julian Grenfell* (1976) by Nicholas Mosley

No. 12   *It's Hard to be Hip over Thirty and Other Tragedies of Married Life* (1968) by Judith Viorst

No. 13   *Consequences* (1919) by E. M. Delafield

No. 14   *Farewell Leicester Square* (1941) by Betty Miller

No. 15   *Tell It to a Stranger: Stories from the 1940s* by Elizabeth Berridge

No. 16   *Saplings* (1945) by Noel Streatfeild

No. 17   *Marjory Fleming* (1946) by Oriel Malet

No. 18   *Every Eye* (1956) by Isobel English

No. 19   *They Knew Mr. Knight* (1934) by Dorothy Whipple

No. 20   *A Woman's Place: 1910–1975* by Ruth Adam

No. 21   *Miss Pettigrew Lives for a Day* (1938) by Winifred Watson

No. 22   *Consider the Years 1938–1946* by Virginia Graham

No. 23   *Reuben Sachs* (1888) by Amy Levy

No. 24   *Family Roundabout* (1948) by Richmal Crompton

No. 25 *The Montana Stories* (1921) by Katherine Mansfield

No. 26 *Brook Evans* (1928) by Susan Glaspell

No. 27 *The Children Who Lived in a Barn* (1938) by Eleanor Graham

No. 28 *Little Boy Lost* (1949) by Marghanita Laski

No. 29 *The Making of a Marchioness* (1901) by Frances Hodgson Burnett

No. 30 *Kitchen Essays* (1922) by Agnes Jekyll

No. 31 *A House in the Country* (1944) by Jocelyn Playfair

No. 32 *The Carlyles at Home* (1965) by Thea Holme

No. 33 *The Far Cry* (1949) by Emma Smith

No. 34 *Minnie's Room: the Peacetime Stories of Mollie Panter-Downes 1947–65*

No. 35 *Greenery Street* (1925) by Denis Mackail

No. 36 *Lettice Delmer* (1958) by Susan Miles

No. 37 *The Runaway* (1872) by Elizabeth Anna Hart

No. 38 *Cheerful Weather for the Wedding* (1932) by Julia Strachey

No. 39 *Manja* (1939) by Anna Gmeyner

No. 40 *The Priory* (1939) by Dorothy Whipple

No. 41 *Hostages to Fortune* (1933) by Elizabeth Cambridge

No. 42 *The Blank Wall* (1947) by Elisabeth Sanxay Holding

No. 43 *The Wise Virgins* (1914) by Leonard Woolf

No. 44 *Tea with Mr Rochester* (1949) by Frances Towers

No. 45 *Good Food on the Aga* (1933) by Ambrose Heath

No. 46 *Miss Ranskill Comes Home* (1946) by Barbara Euphan Todd

No. 47 *The New House* (1936) by Lettice Cooper

No. 48 *The Casino* (1948) by Margaret Bonham

No. 49 *Bricks and Mortar* (1932) by Helen Ashton

No. 50 *The World That Was Ours* (1967) by Hilda Bernstein

No. 51 *Operation Heartbreak* (1950) by Duff Cooper

No. 52 *The Village* (1952) by Marghanita Laski

No. 53 *Lady Rose and Mrs Memmary* (1937) by Ruby Ferguson

No. 54 *They Can't Ration These* (1940) by Vicomte de Mauduit

No. 55 *Flush* (1933) by Virginia Woolf

No. 56 *They Were Sisters* (1943) by Dorothy Whipple

No. 57 *The Hopkins Manuscript* (1939) by R C Sherriff

No. 58 *Hetty Dorval* (1947) by Ethel Wilson

No. 59 *There Were No Windows* (1944) by Norah Hoult

No. 60 *Doreen* (1946) by Barbara Noble

No. 61 *A London Child of the 1870s* (1934) by Molly Hughes

No. 62 *How to Run your Home without Help* (1949)
by Kay Smallshaw

No. 63 *Princes in the Land* (1938) by Joanna Cannan

No. 64 *The Woman Novelist and Other Stories* (1946)
by Diana Gardner

No. 65 *Alas, Poor Lady* (1937) by Rachel Ferguson

No. 66 *Gardener's Nightcap* (1938) by Muriel Stuart

No. 67 *The Fortnight in September* (1931) by RC Sherriff

No. 68 *The Expendable Man* (1963) by Dorothy B Hughes

No. 69 *Journal of Katherine Mansfield* (1927)

No. 70 *Plats du Jour* (1957) by Patience Gray and
Primrose Boyd.

No. 71 *The Shuttle* (1907) by Frances Hodgson Burnett

No. 72 *House-Bound* (1942) by Winifred Peck

No. 73 *The Young Pretenders* (1895) by Edith Henrietta Fowler

No. 74 *The Closed Door and Other Stories* by Dorothy Whipple

No. 75 *On the Other Side: Letters to my Children from Germany
1940–46* by Mathilde Wolff-Mönckeberg

The first Persephone Classics are:
No. 3, No. 8 and No. 21

If you have enjoyed this Persephone book, why not telephone, email or write to us for a free copy of the *Persephone Catalogue*, which gives more information about each of the Persephone Originals and Classics?

PERSEPHONE BOOKS LTD
59 Lamb's Conduit Street
London WC1N 3NB

Telephone: 020 7242 9292
Fax: 020 7242 9272
sales@persephonebooks.co.uk
www.persephonebooks.co.uk